HAVEN 8
by Misty Vixen

D1528057

CHAPTER ONE

He was having a nightmare of some kind, and his head was a throb of pain that renewed itself with an electric shock of agony every few seconds or so.

David had an impression of people screaming, fires burning, ashes and embers and smoke spraying into the hot night air.

He caught ghost images of muzzle flare and then someone's head snapped back in a spray of blood as the life was blown out of them.

He heard someone screaming his name.

Gunfire, so much gunfire.

Then darkness.

...

There were more nightmares, and more confusion.

An incoherent miasma of pain, shot through with anxiety and fear.

In his head, he saw Cait, and Ellie, and Evie, and April. He saw many others. Sometimes hurt. Sometimes captured.

Sometimes dead.

He couldn't tell what was real and what was nightmare.

He drifted for what might have been hours or weeks.

Darkness came, again and again.

...

"Cait!"

David sat bolt upright, grimacing in pain as he moved and immediately began to survey the area around him. He had no idea where he was and yet...it was familiar. Somehow. Inside. He was inside a building. His abused mind hunted fervently for details, but mostly just to see Cait. Cait's beautiful, pale, smiling face.

He sought her reassuring presence, the way he did when he was having nightmares some nights and he would wake up from them and she would be there, or someone would be there to comfort him, to hold him, kiss him, tell him he was safe, make love with him until they both had come and then were pulled back down into sleep.

"David."

Someone *was* here. Someone familiar.

He heard footfalls behind him and twisted around, staggering to his feet.

"David, no, don't try to stand–" Evie said.

Too late. He cried out as he collapsed into a heap on whatever he'd been laying atop. It felt like a nest of blankets and pillows. His whole body ached, but mostly his head hurt. He winced, getting to his hands and knees.

"David, please," Evie said as she crouched beside him. "You need to drink this."

"Cait? Where's Cait? Where's April?" he asked, panting, gasping almost.

"*Drink this, David,*" Evie insisted, a bottle of lukewarm water being held up in front of him. He took it because he wanted to know the answers to his questions, but also because he suddenly felt like he was dying of thirst. Hunger, too. And he had to piss terribly. He rearranged himself in a sitting position, then downed the entire bottle of water.

"Where?" he demanded after he'd finished.

"I think they were taken, I can't know for sure," Evie replied, sounding as worried as he felt. He looked at her. She looked pale and messy and miserable.

"What happened?" he asked, his head spinning.

He remembered...finishing preliminary work on the new settlement. Celebrating. Then...someone shouting his name outside.

And then...

"We were attacked. By the Marauders. A lot of them. David, look at me...it's been two days," Evie said carefully.

He blinked several times. "What?" he managed.

"You've been unconscious for two days."

He blinked several more times. Then he looked around. "Where are we?"

She sighed heavily. "Right back where we started," she said. "You remember that cabin we first went to after the fire? Before there was anyone else, and it was just you and me? This is where we first made love. Right here in this spot, actually," she added, looking down.

That was why it was familiar, he realized.

Yes, this was it. The cabin they'd run to in the night, the basement. As he stared at the nest of blankets and pillows he'd been laying on, he remembered. Last month, he and Evie had walked here, decided to use the place as an emergency outpost, just in case. They'd set up a new 'nest' as it were, and christened it by fucking.

"Who else is here?" he asked.

She shook her head. "It's just you and me."

He groaned, his head still aching. "I need some painkillers," he muttered. "And to take a piss." He slowly got up. Evie helped him.

"I'll get you some painkillers," she said.

He took a moment to get his bearings, his head still spinning in more than one way. The Marauders had attacked them? Yes, he remembered now. He'd stepped out and gotten smashed in the head right away. God, two days? So much must have happened.

"What about the others?" he muttered.

"I don't know most of it," Evie admitted as she came back with a trio of painkillers and another bottle of water in hand.

"Thanks...uh, give me a minute," he said.

"Where are you going?" she asked.

"I'm going to go upstairs and take a leak...is it safe?" he asked.

"Yeah, for now. I was just up there taking a look. You want me to come with you?" she asked.

"No, I need a minute." He hesitated, then he swallowed the three pills and walked over to her. He gave her a hug and a kiss. "Thank you for saving my life. I love you so much, Evie."

"I love you too," she whispered, hugging him tight. "I'm so glad you're awake. I was so fucking scared."

"I'm sorry I didn't wake up sooner," he said.

She laughed softly. "Me too. But you're awake, that's what matters." As he pulled back from the hug, she gave him a stern look. "*Don't* pick at your head wound. I managed to stitch it. Just a few and they're holding, but don't fuck with them, okay?"

"I won't," he promised. "I'll be right back."

He went up the stairs as quickly but as stealthily as possible, the urge to piss overwhelming now. He made his way through the darkness, the only light coming from a collection of candles she had lit downstairs. As he went around to the next set of stairs that would take him to the surface, he was bathed in almost total darkness. He saw no sunlight filtering in through beneath the crack. Which meant it must be night right now.

His head still going this way and that, David focused on the door ahead of him and the task of taking a leak. He had to get grounded. He could feel the immensity of what lay before him, something so vast he couldn't comfortably comprehend it, like looking out at an ocean that you needed to sail across. It would be a long, difficult journey. But before he could even begin to take it, he needed to come back to reality.

David opened the door. It creaked and he winced, but in the faint moonlight filtering into the top portion of the cabin, he saw nothing stirring. He walked slowly around it, keeping his movements cautious and careful, and peered out each window in turn. He saw nothing out there but moonlit trees. No movement. Somewhere in the far distance, he thought he could hear gunfire of some sort, but it might be his imagination. Besides that, just the call of the occasional owl, and a wolf howling somewhere.

Jesus fucking hell, what a nightmare.

He opened the back door and, after looking around once more, his eyes already adjusting well to the near darkness, he pissed. It was a long, long piss and he hadn't felt something so physically relieving in what seemed like a long time.

Two *days*.

Shit.

Last time he'd been out that long was when he'd been bit by a viper.

He had to have pissed himself at some point, or

maybe Evie had gotten him to piss into a bucket or something. He had extremely vague, incoherent memories of laying in that bedding and her talking to him.

Fuck, two days.

He finished up and then drank most of the second bottle of water. What was left, he poured on his face, helping him focus and wake up. He rubbed his eyes, stared out into the dark woodlands that surrounded the cabin. It seemed impossible to think that it was less than a year since he'd first come to this place with Evie, back during the beginning of last winter. For a long moment, he thought, considering the dates, the time that had passed. He couldn't be sure, but it would be roughly seven months ago that River View had burned down.

Seven months?

It felt like seven goddamned years now.

So much had happened to him, he'd changed so much.

David shook his head, then regretted it, mildly. It hurt, but it helped him focus. Focus, that was the key here.

Because he had things to do. So many things.

Turning around, feeling his brain and his body beginning to fully come back online as he started sorting out what lay of him, he headed back downstairs. He found Evie sitting in the only chair large enough for her.

"Okay honey, tell me *exactly* what's been happening? Starting with when I got knocked out," he said as he pulled a seat up next to her and sat down.

She nodded. "Honestly, it was really crazy. There was an attack on the new settlement. I did some fighting, we all did. But it became clear to me that they were outnumbering us, and I saw you. You were passed out. Everything was just chaos and I just...I grabbed you. And ran. I barely even remember doing it. I just ran and ran and ran. I know that they were attacking Haven, too. I remember that. I ran until I ended up here. I don't know why I came here. I brought you to the basement. For a little while I was so fucking scared you had died. But you were still alive. I treated your wounds and kept waiting for you to wake up..."

She took a deep breath and calmed herself, looking up and blinking several times, trying not to cry. He reached out and took her hand. She gripped his hand and squeezed tightly. "I wanted to head out, to help. There was a lot of fighting. A lot. But I couldn't just leave you here. I stayed with you through that first night and all of the first day. You woke up a few times but you were really out of it. During the second night, Ellie showed up. She almost shot me, I didn't think she expected to find anyone here."

"Where'd she go?" he asked. Obviously she wasn't here any longer.

"She was...a little feral," Evie replied uncomfortably. "Her eyes were...I don't know. She was scary. She had blood on her and several guns. She told me to stay put and she'd kill them all. I tried to get some information out of her, but she just told me to stay here and she ran off. I haven't seen her since. The next day, today, well, earlier today, Akila showed up. I was out checking for signs of life, and she showed up. She came and checked on you. She was...a lot more calm and cool than Ellie was, but I guess that's no surprise. She said..." Evie hesitated.

"Yes?" he pressed.

"She said they had Haven and the new settlement completely on lockdown. They had most of our people prisoner. She said she saw Jennifer at Haven, but she hadn't seen Cait or April or Lara. And I asked."

"What about Lima Company? What about the farmers? The fishers?"

She shook her head. "Nothing on them. Akila left, told me to stay here. She was going to hunt them down, that she was perfect at this."

David sighed softly and looked at the candles. At the way the flames flickered and danced. He was silent for several long moments, processing this information, his mind finally calming, settling, clearing.

When he looked back at Evie, he felt different.

"Okay," he said, then he let go of her hand and stood up.

"Okay what?" she asked as he marched across the room.

"I'm going to war," he replied simply.

"How?" she asked, standing and walking a few steps towards him.

"I'll show you."

He moved to the far corner of the room, in a small section of space between the stairwell and the wall where some old furniture had ended up. He dragged out a few chairs, then a desk, then knelt and reached into the space that was revealed. His hand came up holding a black case. He walked with it back over to the table where they'd been sitting.

"What is this?" Evie murmured.

"Paranoia," he replied. "Justified paranoia, apparently."

He set the case down and cracked it open. Inside

was a set of black tactical armor, a pistol with a silencer, a full medical kit, a knife, and ten magazines of ammo.

"I started setting up a few caches of supplies over the summer," he said as he started taking it out and laying it all on the table. "I traded for the tactical armor with a passing trader last month. I figured in the event of some kind of emergency...of something like *this,* well, I needed to have a cache of stuff ready to go. I'd always intended to have more waiting, but never got around to it. I guess I should be lucky I did this," he muttered.

"David..." Evie said, and he looked up at her. She looked worried, and anxious.

"If you're going to try and tell me not to go out there..."

"No," she said, and a somewhat pained smile came onto her large, beautiful face. "It would be pointless. You're going out there. I know you. I can't stop you. I wouldn't want to. It's going to be dangerous, extremely dangerous, but you're right. We need to be out there. I hate that I've waited here as long as I have. Our friends, our family, our loved ones are out there right now..."

"And we're going to help them," David said.

"I know. But I was gonna say..." she hesitated.

"What?"

"It's selfish."

"Tell me anyway," he said, wondering what she was wanting.

She sighed. "It's so dangerous out there, way more than usual. Anything could happen. I guess...I wanted to have sex. Just in case..."

"One of us dies," he said. She nodded. He looked back at the tactical gear, half in the case, half on the table, then at her. She was right. It was going to be dangerous. It might be the most dangerous thing he'd ever done. "Okay," he said. "Let's make love, then we can wage war."

She smiled. "Thank you."

He laughed. "You're doing me a favor as much as I'm doing you a favor. I *love* having sex with you, Evie."

"I know, I just...you're the most intimate person I've ever been with. It's only been with you, and with Cait and April now, that I've actually felt like making love was, well, making love, and not just, you know, having sex."

"I know how you feel," he said. "Come here, babe."

He stepped up to her and she dipped her head. Her height difference was something that he'd gotten used to, but it was still so obvious to him. Having a girlfriend a full foot and a half taller than you was an interesting experience. She kissed him firmly on the mouth, a long, lingering kiss with a lot of tongue. Then she pulled back and started taking her clothes off. He joined her, stripping out of what he was wearing.

He could make time for this.

Though not a whole lot of it.

He kept worrying about Cait. Was she okay? Was she safe? Was she hurt? And the others? God, so many women, so many people in his life that he cared about now, that he was worried about. He was going to kill for them.

But right now, before the storm came, he was going to enjoy this one, shining moment of peace and serenity with a woman he loved.

It wasn't long before they were naked and

embracing on the nest of blankets. It wasn't the most comfortable place to have sex, but it didn't need to be. Even as Evie settled onto her back and opened her legs for him, and he settled in between her tremendous thighs, he knew it wasn't going to be anything but a quickie.

They didn't have time, and they needed their strength for what was to come. David could tell he was in shitty enough shape as it was. But he wanted this, they both did. Perhaps they needed it to help them come to terms with the war that lay ahead of them. He didn't want to think about that.

And he didn't, not for a little bit, as he slid into her.

"Oh, David..." she whispered as he penetrated her, sliding into that slippery goliath vagina, into her familiar depths. "Oh honey, yes..." she moaned as he began making love to her.

"Evie..." he moaned, laying against her, holding her, embracing her.

As he started to thrust into her, to bury his rock-hard length into her, everything else fell away. He listened to her moaning and panting, to the own sounds coming out of him, to the sound of their skin slapping together.

His cock disappeared into her again and again, and the pleasure burned into him. Both of them were soon panting, and she held him close to her. Held his much smaller frame against her much larger body, enjoying every second of their coupling.

"I love you, David," she whispered, her voice thick with emotion. "I love you."

"I love you too, Evie," he moaned, his own voice hoarse with it as well. "I love you so much. I love you, honey."

They lost themselves in the sex. He thought of nothing for a glorious few minutes but her voluptuous, hot, smooth body and her perfect inhuman vagina and the way it felt to make love with her. The emotions he could feel radiating off of her as intensely as the heat of her body. The way she held him, the way she moved her body against his own, the passion in her voice. Everything felt far more intense than it usually did when they made love.

As such, it didn't last long.

Both of them began to orgasm at almost the same time. They each tried to be quiet, stifling themselves and their intense cries of passion, given that anyone could be nearby. Anyone or anything could overhear them.

David lost himself in that hot release of liquid, his seed spilling out of him into her orgasming vagina. They held each other and moaned in pure sexual gratification, pure loving ecstasy. He quietly moaned her name several times, feeling nothing but absolute love for her, feeling a depth and intensity of love he once had never known and even had questioned the possibility of.

But he knew now. He felt this love for her, for Cait, for April. To varying degrees, the other women in his life who regularly shared his bed.

Women who were out there now, injured or captured or fighting for their lives or…

Possibly even dead.

No, David thought as he came back to himself, forcibly brought back to reality as the orgasm fell away, leaving him panting, *no, I won't think about that.*

He couldn't, and keep his focus.

He had to assume they were all still alive, and

that he could help them.

"I love you sweetheart...but the time to work has come," he murmured.

"I understand," she said. She patted his back once. "I love you, too."

Then she released him. David pulled out of her, and then he began to prepare for the greatest battle he had ever fought.

He found some water that they had stashed there after getting back to his feet and went about the process of cleaning up. It would help him focus, and like the sex he had just had, it might be the last time he got to enjoy it for quite a while.

When they had initially come here, they'd stashed some food, some water, some basic quality of life supplies, some medicine. He soaped and washed and dried, then examined his body. There were a few bruises, but it seemed like the only serious problem was the injury on his head.

"Will you take a look at it for me, love?" he asked, realizing he very well couldn't look at the top of his own head.

"Yes," she replied, coming over. She took a moment to examine the wound, pulling a bandage she'd put in place away. He winced but held his peace. "Let me just clean it really quick, then reapply the bandage. It's looking good. You dizzy?" she asked.

"No," he replied. "Just a headache. Otherwise I'm fine. I'm kind of pumped, honestly."

"Well, you've never had your work so cut out for you," she murmured.

"Maybe," he said. Then he lost some of his enthusiasm. "God, I hope Cait's okay."

"They seemed intent on taking prisoners, that's

what Akila told me. I'm sure she's okay," Evie replied as she came over with the medical supplies.

He didn't say anything, just endured his own unhappy thoughts and the pain of her tending to his wound in silence. She might not be okay. None of them might be. Right now, all he knew for a fact was that Evie was okay.

And even that might change soon.

No. Focus. Had to keep focus.

"Done," she said.

"Thank you."

He walked back over to the table and began pulling on his tactical gear. It was all black. Black boxers and socks, black body armor that was lightweight enough to allow mobility, but should be enough to stop at least a few bullets. He'd been saving it for a rainy day and now it was fucking pouring. He slid it all on, settling it into place, and finished by slipping a black beanie over his head, wincing slightly at the wound.

Next, he secured the spare ammunition in some of the varied pockets. Then he slid the combat knife he'd also secured in the sheath on his thigh. After securing the medical equipment and a canteen that he filled with water, he took a moment to make sure it was all held firmly in place so he didn't make any more noise than necessarily while moving. Cait, Evie, Akila, and Lara had all taught him several things during their time together.

He intended to put it all to good use.

"Wow," Evie said when he finished by lacing up his boots. "You look...different."

"Do I?" he asked.

"Yeah, you look...like a soldier. You look scary, actually. A little like how Ellie looked when I saw her," she said uncomfortably.

"Don't worry, I'm not going feral," he said. "But I fully intend to wipe every last one of these motherfuckers out. They declared war on us. They attacked us. I'm sure they've killed some of us. I swear I saw people dying while you were carrying me out..."

She frowned, nodded. "Yeah. I saw at least two of Val's people shot in the head, and one of our people from Haven was machine-gunned through. Just pumped full of holes..." she whispered.

"This is the kind of thing I've been preparing for. All summer it felt like the other shoe was gonna drop, you remember me saying that?" She nodded. "It's dropped. I've been preparing for this, getting ready for it, and now it's here. I've pissed away two whole days comatose. Ellie and Akila and the others are all out there fighting, and we're going to help them. Whatever it takes, however long it takes, we're getting our people back. Our havens, our friends, our fucking way of life. We're getting it all back."

"I'm with you, David," Evie said, her voice strengthening.

He looked her up and down. She was fully dressed now, her hair pulled into a tight ponytail, a pistol in her hand.

Her expression was grim and determined.

She looked every inch the warrior he knew she could be, when the time called for it.

It had called for it.

He nodded tightly. "Let's get out there and make them regret the day they met us."

CHAPTER TWO

The painkillers were doing their job.

David felt better as he stepped out into the cool night air. Maybe it was the sex, too. And the washing up, and finally putting on that fresh set of tactical gear.

Looking around once more at the trees, the pistol in his hand, David realized that he felt somehow different now. His head had settled, his focus had returned with an intensity he hadn't experienced in some time. His body ached faintly and his head still hurt, though it was distant now. In all the times he'd gone out into the wilderness to hunt men or monsters, to retrieve something, to do some task, he had never felt quite like this.

He felt...

Driven.

He felt like a rifle scope that had been zeroed to perfection, aimed directly at the unmoving head of someone that absolutely needed to die.

"What time is it?" he whispered as they set out slowly from the cabin, heading north, towards the river.

"I'm not sure. After midnight, I think. The sun went down a few hours ago," Evie replied, following in his wake. "Where are we going?"

"The bunker. I stored a lot of guns there, and we're going to need more than a pair of pistols to start taking these assholes down."

"Okay, that makes sense."

They moved through the trees. It was harder for Evie to be silent, given her size and the fact that she didn't have as much practice moving stealthily. He let his senses come alive, like he'd learned to do for a long time. You had to learn it if you intended to survive.

He'd picked it up for years, but he hadn't truly begun to hone it and file it down into something sharp and dangerous until the last few months or so, when he realized that he was going to have to take survival a lot more seriously when he'd helped establish Haven.

He'd trained with Ellie, and Cait, and then Akila and Lara later.

They were all far better than he was, perhaps than he ever would be. But he was a hell of a lot better than he had been at moving quietly, at listening to his surroundings, at knowing when someone or something was around, lurking, looking for a kill. At this moment, as he moved through the woods with a silenced pistol in his hands, he'd never felt more switched on and ready to act. For the moment, he just wanted to get to that bunker.

Ellie's paranoia had infected him at some point. He remembered taking several trips with her across the region after dealing with the viper threat. They'd visited her stashes, making sure they were decently supplied, and establishing a few more. They'd managed to rig the bunker to a code that only he and a few others knew, and he'd put a stash of guns down there. He'd love to get his hands on some explosives and a nice slick assault rifle to help him deal with these assholes. He glanced at Evie as they moved on through the trees and the darkness.

"What can you tell me about them?" he asked, keeping his voice low.

"There's a *lot* of them. Hundreds, I think. They all wore that black leather, they were all armed, and they seemed pretty well-coordinated. Much more of a fighting force than those assholes we had to take down over winter. These guys seem like an actual, serious threat. Akila told me they were moving teams of people across the land, sweeping the forests and fields for runaways."

"Why are they doing this?" David muttered.

"I was thinking about that. I imagine it's how they expand their forces. They take over a region with a show of force, lock up the survivors, kill the toughest as a message to the others, break the new people and induct them into their army."

"Fuck," David whispered. "They fucked up, coming here."

"Yes," Evie said flatly, "they did."

A few minutes later, they came to the edge of the forest. He could hear the river nearby, a comforting, familiar sound he'd grown fond of over the last seven months. They crouched at the treeline, waiting. He looked both ways. In the far distance, he thought he could see some lights to the left, towards the new settlement. It had to be the gas station area he'd first met Amanda and her family at all those many months ago. Almost certainly there was a contingent of the Marauders there, waiting to trap anyone that came by, no doubt.

"Okay, come on. Nice and easy, we're gonna cross here," he murmured.

"Are you sure?" Evie asked.

"Yes. You see that stunted tree there?" he asked, pointing over the road and across the thirty or so feet to the river.

She squinted. "Yeah."

"I checked it out. The river gets pretty narrow there, and there's a big log across it. Should hold," he said.

"I hope you're right or I'm gonna make a big fucking splash," she muttered.

"We can do this. Come on."

They broke away from the treeline after double-checking the area one more time, then crossed the road. They kept as low as they could, moving as quickly as stealth would allow them. They kept going, crossing the grassy area, until they reached the stunted tree. He was worried the log wouldn't be there anymore, but it was. Solid and sturdy.

"Cover me," he whispered, holstering the pistol so he didn't drop it in the water.

"Check," Evie replied, her own pistol ready.

He stepped up onto the log. Tested his weight against it. Still seemed steady. He began making his way across it. The log felt solid enough under his feet as he made his way across it, though he'd be lying if didn't admit to hunching up slightly, expecting a bullet to come out of the darkness and punch through his skull. But he reached the other side without a problem. David pulled his pistol back out and secured the area beyond, seeing nothing but trees. The wind whispered through the trees, sending them all swaying.

"Come on," he said quietly, turning back around and covering her.

Evie stepped up to the log and put one foot on it, put some weight on it, then some more, then put the other foot on it.

The log shifted, very slightly.

She swallowed, looking at him, then looking around again.

"I've got you covered," he whispered.

She nodded and took another step. Then another.

When it didn't shift any further, she moved a bit faster. David kept a sharp eye out for any Marauders or undead that might be sneaking up on them, but he didn't see anything.

Suddenly, the log lurched beneath Evie's feet. She let out a sound of shock that she managed to cut off quickly, struggling to keep her balance. David was frozen in indecision for a second, unsure if he could get to her in time to help catch her and not even being sure he could if he managed it, and then she settled, regaining her balance.

She laughed softly, then finished coming over.

"People say goliaths are clumsy," she muttered.

"You aren't clumsy, love," David replied.

"Yep. Come on. Let's keep going."

She pulled her pistol back out and they headed off into the next treeline.

...

They were heading into stalker territory.

It was eerie and unnerving, moving through the forest at night. Even though he'd done it several times, it still bugged him. He and Ellie and, later, he and Akila had gone on several night hunts together. Sometimes all three of them went. Mostly it was just to go have sex in new places, but it was also about teaching him to be able to move and stay alive at night. He was deeply grateful for those trips now.

Were they still alive?

Well, if anyone was, it would probably be them. They were exceptionally skilled at staying alive. Of course, maybe not, given that they were both huntresses, and they would put themselves in danger more often than not.

As they moved through the dark forest, the night was broken by a flare-up of gunfire somewhere off towards the lake. Somewhere in their neck of the woods. David and Evie halted, listening, trying to determine what, exactly, was happening. But it was too indistinct beyond the fact that several machine guns were chattering away. Maybe a Marauder team had run into a pack of stalkers. He hoped so. They deserved a lot worse.

In a way, he was itching to run into some of them. David didn't think of himself as bloodthirsty, but he'd defended himself enough, had his life and the lives of those he loved threatened enough that he was familiar with killing by now. Undead and alive. The undead never bothered him, they were more like shells. Animals at worst, monsters at best. He felt worse killing a deer for its meat than he did putting down a stalker or a ripper. And although he'd never be completely comfortable with ending a life, he knew it was necessary sometimes.

Right now, it was very necessary.

He could still hear people screaming from that first attack. Still hear gunfire. Still had flashes of bodies he'd caught glimpses of as he'd been carried out of the new settlement in Evie's arms, struggling, and failing, to swim back to full consciousness.

There it was.

He saw the large clearing that the bunker was built into. Hard to believe it wasn't too long ago that he and Ellie and Cait had stood atop that bunker and first faced a horde of stalkers and then faced down Stern when he'd come and saved their asses, just to rob them. Then again, half a year could be a long time. Now, he saw nothing in the field. Just a carpet of grass and the occasional lump of a bush or patch of flowers in the moonlight.

And the dark mound in the center of the clearing.

He frowned as he thought he saw something wrong with the bunker, but he couldn't be sure from this distance.

"Okay, let's do this," he muttered. "We get the guns and get out."

"Then where?" she asked.

"I'm still considering that," he replied.

"I'm ready."

They left the relative safety of the forest after seeing nothing obviously threatening in the area, and jogged lightly across the clearing. Again, he expected something to happen. Gunfire to suddenly ring out, bullets to smash into him, *something*. But the night remained unbroken and still as they reached the bunker.

He knew their luck couldn't hold out forever, and as he got within sight of the front door, David knew that it had run out.

"Shit," he whispered.

"Damn," Evie said softly as they came to a halt.

The keypad was ripped away, wires exposed and still sparking occasionally. Apparently the Marauders had a tech genius on their roster just like Haven did. Either that or they employed some brute force and got *really* lucky in the process.

"Come on," David grunted as he stepped to the side of the door, activated the small flashlight that was attached to the pistol, and leaned carefully around the edge. He shined the light down the descending stairwell. He saw muddy bootprints on the stairs. Great. He supposed it was possible that someone from his side had gotten in here, but it seemed unlikely. He took the lead, pistol aimed forward and down, held tightly with both hands. Evie backed him up. They descended the stairwell. He listened hard for signs of life.

But the bunker seemed as dead as the first time they'd broken into it.

As they reached the bottom of the stairwell and passed through the door they found there, David found even more signs of pilfering. Trash and mud littered the floor of the main room. Evie stood guard in the main room while David moved quickly in a circle to check out each of the various doorways that led into different parts of the compact underground bunker. Each room was either empty or torn apart for whatever useful supplies and materials had been left in it. He found trash, broken furniture, and empty boxes.

"Fuck," he whispered as he finished searching the last room. "They were here already, and they were thorough. There's nothing left."

"Now what?" she asked.

"There's another cache Ellie and I made northwest of here, maybe twenty minutes' walk away. We'll go there," he replied as he headed for the door, turning off the flashlight. "Then we'll figure out what's what."

He headed up the stairs with Evie in tow again.

As he reached the top, just shy of the threshold, he froze. Evie stopped behind him as he raised a fist. Neither spoke a word or uttered a sound. They waited. Outside, the wind blew and the trees swayed in its current. Somewhere, an owl hooted.

"Thought I heard something," he muttered finally.

It might have been nothing, but he couldn't shake a bad feeling. Then again, he'd had a bad feeling since he'd woken up in the cabin's basement not all that long ago. Readjusting his grip on his pistol, David stepped back out into the moonlight.

He realized his mistake the exact moment a quartet of flashlights snapped to life, to his right, two to his left. At the same time, someone rose up from a prone position directly in front of him. He was holding a shotgun.

They all wore black leather armor.

"Drop the weapon now!" the man in front of him snapped.

David grit his teeth, trying to think of some way out of this. No! He was barely an hour into this fucking thing, he couldn't already be captured or killed!

"Come out of there and drop your weapons, *right now!*" the man ordered.

He dropped his pistol and put his hands up. He could tell they were going to shoot him, maybe not kill him, but definitely shoot him if he didn't drop it. Behind him, he heard Evie's own weapon hit the ground.

To the left, one of the others pulled out a radio. "This is Squad Six, we've captured the human male and the female goliath."

"All right, get down on the ground," the leader said.

As David began to slowly get to his knees, he heard another voice come back over the radio. "What about the blue jag? Or the nymph? We need them caught immediately."

"Still no sign–"

There was a whisper of sound and a flash somewhere far away to his right, something David barely caught out of his peripheral vision. Suddenly, the man holding the radio's head disappeared in a tremendous spray of gore.

"Sniper! Sniper!" the leader screamed as they scattered.

Another distant flash of light and the leader's neck blew out in a huge spray of blood and, David saw in the split second of time that passed, it actually detached his head from his body. David crouched and scooped up his pistol. Twisting to the left, he pumped four rounds into the body of the second flashlight-wielder there, the final round punching though his right eye and turning it into an explosion of blood and brains.

He heard Evie yell in fury and something very solid connect with something else, followed by a sickening crack and a scream.

Another flare from the treeline and he heard a grunt from above him. Turning, David saw that one of the bastards had gotten up onto the roof. Now he was staggering around, holding his shoulder, which was bleeding profusely, his arm hanging at an awful angle.

David finished off the last man on the ground, seeing that Evie had straight punched the second man to the right in the face and probably broken every bone above his neck. The final man toppled over and landed with another awful crack a few feet beside David.

His neck had broken instantly on impact.

For several heartbeats, nothing happened.

Then the radio crackled. "Squad Six, say again, you cut off." A pause. "Squad Six answer me." A shorter pause. "Answer me right now, goddamnit! That's an order!...*fuck!*"

"I see movement," Evie murmured.

David looked. Someone had emerged from the distant treeline, just a bare hint of a figure moving towards them at a light jog. It had to be someone friendly. Ruby, maybe? Wouldn't that be nice. She *was* a sharpshooter...

But as David crouched and snagged up one of the fallen men's weapons, a submachine gun that looked to be in pretty good condition, he looked back up and caught sight of the mysterious figure, and recognized her immediately as she got closer.

"Akila!" he said, relieved to see her.

"David, Evie," she replied, coming to a halt in front of them. She looked around at the bodies, then settled her gaze on Evie. "I thought I told you to stay put."

"He's awake now, and do you really think you can keep us out of the fight?" Evie asked.

Akila pursed her lips, studying David. She had changed, he realized. Or perhaps reverted was more accurate. There was a cold detachment to her now, a sharp lethality in her gaze and her movements and stance.

"Fair enough," she said. "I can't stay, I have more killing to do."

"Wait, wait," David replied quickly, as it looked like she was serious, already getting ready to leave. "You've been running around here for two days, I take it. What have you learned? We need *some* kind of intelligence on the situation."

"Fair enough," she repeated, crouching by one of the bodies and patting it down.

She was completely naked save for a belt and a bandoleer, from which hung a few grenades, some throwing knives, a pair of silenced pistols, and an ammo pouch. A scoped rifle hung across her back. He also saw a combat knife in a sheath strapped to her thigh.

"Both Haven and our new, unnamed settlement are completely under their control. So are the hunting grounds. I think some of Val's people ended up there. I definitely have seen Marauder activity around the farms, but I didn't get an impression of fighting. But there was some fighting at the fishing village."

"What about Lima Company? The doctors?" he asked.

"I haven't had a chance to check on the doctors. I tried to get there twice, but both times got routed by these assholes. As for Lima Company, I have no idea. I haven't seen or heard from them once during this whole thing, but I heard a lot of fighting coming from that direction last night. Could've been unrelated," she replied, grabbing some ammo and another grenade from the body.

"Have you seen Ellie? Lara? Cait?"

"No, I haven't seen anyone friendly. Although I have found signs of Ellie's handiwork. Anyway, I have to go. I'm on a roll and the more of these monsters I can kill, the fewer we'll have to deal with when we eventually deal with them." She paused after securing the last of the gear she'd pulled from the dead Marauders, then stepped closer to them.

"I love you, David," she said, pulling him into a tight hug and kissing him on the mouth.

"I love you, Evie," she said, doing the same with their goliath friend.

They both told her they loved her as well, and then, after wishing them luck, she slipped off into the darkness like the assassin she evidently was.

"She's frightening, I have to admit," David murmured.

"Good thing she loves us," Evie replied.

He looked at another one of the corpses, knelt, and began patting it down. "Let's finish this up, we need to get a move on too."

...

David tried to do something with the latest bit of information he'd been given by Akila before she'd raced off into the darkness to kill and maim. Unfortunately, there wasn't much. It sounded like the farmers had either been utterly dominated or some kind of deal had been struck. Given how Thatch and his people had been reluctant to stay out of conflicts before, and the fact that he had a powerful bargaining chip, he thought it was very likely that they had negotiated some kind of surrender in return for keeping his people safe.

David couldn't even bring himself to be angry at the man. Although he'd been out or gone for most of it, the flashes he got of the battle at the new settlement had been brutal. So that was going to be a problem.

The fishing village...

He'd need to see for sure, but maybe they'd put up a brief fight and then realized they couldn't make it and they should try to save their people while they still could. Hell, maybe that's what had happened at Haven, too.

So where the fuck was Stern and Lima Company?

He'd hardly spoken to any of them for weeks, but this was like the *exact* type of thing they had been preparing for and guarding against! Maybe they were out there fighting guerrilla warfare style, just like

Ellie and Akila and now him and Evie. Or maybe the Marauders had done their research and taken out Lima Company first.

Although…

Something nagged at him as he made his way through the forest, heading towards the watchtower that he and Katya had once ascended and surveyed the land from, north of the hospital. He intended to gather up some more supplies, (the SMG and the spare ammo was nice, but not enough for what he had in mind), and then go straight to the hospital.

He was beginning to put together some kind of plan in his head, but he absolutely required more than just himself and Evie. He was kind of mad at Akila for just leaving, but maybe she was right.

Maybe, for now, she'd do her best operating solo.

He froze again and dropped into a crouch, aiming the pistol with both hands into the dim moonlight again. They were deep in the woods now and he heard heavy breathing, running. Someone was coming towards them and not being subtle about it.

"Get her! Now!" someone shouted.

Fuck! Had to be a friendly being chased by the Marauders. He made a quick motion to Evie, who nodded and slid into place behind a particularly large tree. They were coming from the west, from the direction of the hospital. David could see lights shining, flashlights swaying wildly. He kept out of sight as much as he could, staring intently, studying the situation. They were going to be right on his position and shortly.

Three flashlights, but the person being chased didn't have one.

He licked his lips and got his pistol ready. The SMG didn't have a silencer. Roughly parallel to

Evie's position, he pressed his side against a tree and waited.

He heard panting and frightened sounds that he recognized immediately, but couldn't place in the heat of the moment.

Someone cursed.

"Stop!" another voice, a woman, shouted angrily.

"Get the *fuck* back here bitch!" a third voice snarled angrily.

A slim figure raced between him and Evie, too fast to see clearly, and then the flashlight-wielding bastards came through. David aimed and caught a lucky shot, sending a bullet punching into the skull of one of the three Marauders. He let out part of a startled yelp that was immediately cut off and then collapsed into a tangle of rolling limbs like a puppet with its strings cut right off. The other two skidded to a halt, turning to find their attackers.

"What the fuck!?" the female Marauder demanded.

Evie shot her in the face.

The third survivor had spotted David fast and was drawing a bead on him, but David was faster. He shot the man twice in the face.

"Come back!" David called. "Whoever you are, come back! You're safe!"

The sound of running slowed to a halt, then suddenly started up again, this time running back. Who was it? He knew he should know, but he was too pumped full of adrenaline to put together the tiny fragments of pieces he'd already received so far.

Abruptly, a slender green figure emerged from the way she'd run, stepping into one of the fallen flashlight's beams.

It was April.

"David!" she cried, and threw herself into his arms.

CHAPTER THREE

"April, are you okay?" David asked as he hugged her tightly against himself with one arm, while keeping the pistol at ready with the other.

"I-I'm not hurt," she whispered. "Just so fucking scared. Oh my God."

"Get your breath back, honey," he said, giving her a little squeeze.

But he felt bad, because he felt the press of time, the need to do *something*. Not to mention, every moment they stood here was another moment potential foes drew closer.

"The hospital," she said. "They took over the hospital!"

David cursed softly. "Is anyone hurt? Dead?"

"I don't know, I don't think so. Vanessa wasn't there, though. Everyone else was there. The assholes attacked a little while ago. They took over. Katya slipped me out the back and told me to go find help. I tried sneaking away, but then some of them saw me and started coming after me..." She looked down at the three corpses.

"Okay, we have to go rescue them," David said.

"I...I don't know..." April whispered, still breathing heavily.

"April," he said, stepping back from her and looking her in the eyes. "Breathe."

She stared at him, still panting, then blinked a few times. She took a deep breath, closed her eyes, held it, then let it out slowly. She opened her eyes.

"I'm...I'm okay," she said softly.

He was impressed. All her time at Haven and among the others must have done wonders to help her confidence.

"Okay, grab a gun," he said, crouching at the nearest corpse and looking it over.

They were all carrying pistols, it seemed, and none better than the model he had. He took one of them anyway and tucked it down the back of his pants after making sure it was fully loaded. April picked up one of the other pistols that had been dropped.

"I'm ready," she said.

"I want you to keep back and watch our six, okay?" he asked.

She nodded. "I can do that."

"Good. I need to know, how many were there?" he asked.

"I'm not sure. At least a dozen, maybe more," she replied.

"All right, this is what we're going to do. I'm going to go to the front and distract them. You two are going to try and slip through the back. When you start shooting, I'll start shooting, and hopefully we'll take them by surprise. If Katya's in there, I know she'll jump at any opportunity, no matter how tiny, to kill them. We've gotta do it fast before they can get reinforcements in."

"David, I don't like this," Evie murmured.

"I fucking hate it, but we don't have a lot of options right now. We *need* to get people to safety and get some allies. We need a plan beyond the guerrilla warfare that Akila and Ellie are pulling," David replied.

"They're okay?" April asked.

"We saw Akila ten minutes ago. She insists on staying alone. Don't know about Ellie. I just woke up from a two-day coma apparently," David replied.

"I was so worried about you and the others, I had

no idea where you all were..."

"What happened to you?" David asked as they walked towards the hospital, keeping his voice low.

"I was in Haven when they attacked. I was there until this evening. Some of the others made a distraction and I managed to get out. I think some of the others did too, but I'm not sure. Jennifer's still there. Lara was there, but this morning they took a group of people to the other settlement and she was among them. I don't know why. I tried to go to the farmers, but I saw that there were those assholes in black leather around, so I decided to go to the hospital. But it was *such* a long walk. There were a lot of patrols around. Sometimes I had to hide for half an hour at a stretch. But I finally got there. They didn't really know what was happening," she said.

"All right...quiet," David whispered.

He could see the lights of the hospital up ahead. They were one of the buildings that actually had a generator, and apparently the Marauders had made use of it, turning some of the exterior lights on. Great. They stopped a good fifty feet away.

"Make a wide circle around back. I'll give you a three minute count. Try to keep it straight in your head and I'll do the same. When three minutes are up, I'll go 'negotiate'. Wait, here." He traded pistols with April. "Use that silencer. You remember everything I taught you about shooting?"

"Yeah, I remember," she said quietly.

He gave her a firm hug and a kiss on the mouth. "I love you, April. You can do this."

She trembled, once, then her expression hardened somewhat. "I love you too, David." She paused, took a deep breath, let it out. "I can do this."

"I'll be there with you," Evie said.

"Good luck."

"You too."

He and Evie shared one more kiss and then they were off. David crept to the edge of the treeline beside the old abandoned building that had become the hospital, trying to keep a three minute count in his head as accurate as possible. He could hear people talking, and someone shouting inside the building. It sounded like Katya.

Fuck, she must be furious right now.

The countdown in his head finished and David made himself start walking down along the path towards the entrance. He could hear two voices, people talking, though he couldn't be sure what they were discussing.

"Hello?" he called.

Both voices immediately stopped.

"Who the fuck's that?!" one of them snapped.

At the same time, he heard someone knocking and saying, "We've got someone out here."

"My name is David, I'm the leader of the settlement known as Haven," he said, hoping to draw a lot of attention his way.

By now, if there was a rear guard, Evie and April would have taken him out. And if the people inside were smart, then the second they were warned about someone appearing in the front, they'd send someone to check the back.

Unless they were distracted by an important target.

"Come out with your hands up! Now!" the first voice said.

"I'm coming out. I want to negotiate," he replied evenly, walking down the path.

He took his time. The path was lined with plants,

all of it thick with vegetation now. Back during winter, he remembered hiding among the dead trees while Cait did basically this exact same thing. They'd mowed down some of the assholes trying to shake down the hospital. Now he was going to do the same damn thing.

Hopefully.

David emerged in the harsh lights lit along the front. Two people were standing out front. They wore black leather and held submachine guns. Someone was standing up top in the window that Katya or Vanessa usually greeted him from, holding an assault rifle.

"Throw your weapons down, right now," one of the Marauders said flatly.

Three weapons covered him as he carefully tossed the submachine gun away, out of reach, and then did the same with his one visible pistol.

"Let me talk to your leader. You people have invaded our land and this is absolutely a hostile action. If your leader agrees to leave now and never return, then we'll call it even," David said. He was surprised at how calm his voice sounded.

One of them stared at him with an incredulous look. He lowered his SMG. "Are you fucking shitting me?"

"You have *no* idea who you are fucking with," David replied, and the anger he felt didn't need to be faked at all. "You have *no fucking clue* what a giant pile of *shit* you have stepped into coming here and doing this. If you don't *all* leave right now, then *none* of you are leaving. Do you fucking understand me?" he growled.

Maybe it was something in his eyes or the way he was actually trembling with fury, but one of the men out front took a step back.

"That's not how this works. We have control. There's no arguing with it," the first man who had spoken said, largely unmoved. "But the boss wants you for sure. Don't move and—"

Suddenly, a spray of gunfire sounded off within the structure.

"What the fuck!?" the man up top, in the window, snapped, turning away.

Someone was shouting. Then several someones were shouting.

In the second that the two men looked back towards the door, which was just beginning to open up, David reached back, tore the pistol he'd stuffed down the back of his pants loose, and emptied the entire magazine into the two fuckers standing guard out front.

They screamed as the bullets ripped into their bodies, the leather armor only stopping some of them. Blood splashed across the front of the hospital as they crashed to the ground. David dropped the pistol as it clicked empty and dove for his submachine gun.

As he snatched it up, the man in the window suddenly returned.

"Freeze!" he screamed, aiming his own piece down at David.

David snapped the SMG up and fired, hosing the window down with bullets. The Marauder's scream was cut off as a round went into his mouth and punched through his head and out the back of his skull. David could feel the impact of several bullets in the earth near him as the man had returned fire, the last few rounds spitting out as his nerves twitched spasmodically. He heard chaos inside the building and prayed that his friends were going to be okay.

People were screaming, gunfire was roaring as several guns sounded off.

As he got to his feet and prepared to charge the front entrance, another Marauder suddenly appeared in the open doorway.

David froze. The guy had him dead to rights, pistol aimed right at him.

Suddenly, the man's face blew away and came apart in a horrific spray of blood and brains and skull fragments as someone fired a shotgun point-blank into the back of his head. His body took a single, staggering step forward and then collapsed. Katya appeared behind him, holding a shotgun, racking it, and she aimed at David.

She nearly shot him, too, but stopped at the last second.

"David! Fuck! Get in here!" she snapped, looking to the left and then right, covering him.

He hurried over and she stepped out of the way to let him in. Once he was inside, she slammed the door shut and locked it. He looked around the main room where three more Marauders lay dead. Janice, the jag nurse, was there, a pistol in her hand and a fierce look on her face. April was walking into the room from the back, looking dazed. Evie came in behind her. He heard more commotion from deeper inside.

"Is that all of them?" he asked.

"You killed the guy upstairs?" Katya replied. He nodded. "Yeah, that's all of them then," she said as she walked over to the nearest body and started patting it down. "They do radio check-ins roughly every hour. Last radio check-in was half an hour ago, which means we've got maybe half an hour to play with here *if* no one was around to hear that fucking mess. Where the *fuck* have you been?" she snapped.

"Comatose," David replied.

She glanced at him, then grunted and went back to her search.

"Everyone in here!" David called.

"Janice, go be lookout," Katya said as she finished her first search and shifted over to the next corpse.

"Yep," the jag replied tightly. She got up and jogged towards the stairs.

The others filtered into the room, looking dazed for the most part. Donald came in, a hand to his head, which was bleeding. The two youngest of the group followed after him, the nurses. Amanda, who looked as frightened as he'd seen her the first time they'd met, and Peter, a young jag man who was holding his right bicep and wincing.

"You're shot?" David asked.

"Just a graze," he muttered, sitting down in one of the chairs.

"Where's Vanessa?" Evie asked.

"She left earlier today," Katya replied. "What the *fuck* is going on out there?"

"You don't know?" David asked.

"April just showed up and tried to update us, and she wasn't exactly coherent in her delivery. We heard the shooting two nights ago and wanted to go check it out, but Donald wanted to stay put," she growled, her sharp gaze cutting angrily to the older man.

He said nothing in his own defense, just sat there, looking a bit dazed still.

"So we stayed put, waiting for someone to come to us, until finally Vanessa had had enough. She left about twelve hours ago. We haven't heard from her since. April shows up, and then *these* fucks," she snapped, her face screwing up in anger as she delivered a swift kick to the nearest corpse, "showed up."

"They're called Marauders," David said. "They've taken over the entire region. I was knocked silly in the initial attack on our new settlement. Evie got me to a cabin where I was basically comatose until about two hours ago. So far, all we've seen is April and Akila."

"What's that bad bitch doing?" Katya muttered.

"Killing. She's gone all rogue assassin on us, which is probably for the best. We need people out there, causing confusion and chaos while I figure out how the fuck we're going to handle this," David replied.

"And how exactly are we going to handle this?" Donald asked, speaking up for the first time.

"First thing is first, we *need* a place we can safely send people to. Non-combatants and wounded. Somewhere the Marauders can't easily get to them..." he muttered.

"Can't be here, they already know about this," Katya said. "Where the *fuck's* Lima Company?"

"No idea," he replied.

"The settlements are out," Evie said. "Seems like they own them all."

Where could this possibly be? This was the first big thing they needed to crack, because he needed to be able to get people safe and somewhere out of the way, so he could wage war without worrying as much.

He thought of several isolated locations he'd come across during his adventures. The abandoned cabins and houses? The old railway station he'd once fought a bunch of rippers in with Cait? Those trailers he'd first found Lindsay in? The quarry? No, those were all too easy to get to. Obviously these people had done their research and recon, but where was somewhere they couldn't easily get to or might not think of?

The factory? Maybe...the only other place out that far was–

David's eyes widened. "Oh my God," he whispered as a plan suddenly snapped together in his head, coalescing immediately.

"What?" several of them replied at once.

"I know where we can get people. It'll be a pain, but I think it can work."

"Where?" Katya asked.

He opened his mouth to respond, then hesitated, looking around. He looked down at one of the corpses, which was holding a radio. It seemed to be off, but he felt paranoia creeping in. Was someone somehow listening in on them?

Katya followed his gaze. She reached down and snatched the radio up. Shit, why hadn't David thought to do that last time?

"I can show you," he said. "It'll be a bit of a walk."

"Everyone get ready to go," Katya said. She moved over to Donald. "Come on, let's look at that head wound. Someone help Peter with his wound."

"I can do it," Amanda murmured.

"Five minutes people," David said. "Arm yourselves and grab whatever you need, you've got exactly five minutes before we move."

...

"I'm not going with you," Katya said as they all

headed out of the hospital.

"*What?*" David replied, temporarily frozen by surprise.

That was the last thing he'd expected to hear. Katya had a hard look on her rough, violently beautiful face. She now wore a bulletproof vest and some cargo pants and heavy black boots. She had two pistols, a shotgun across her back, and was wielding an assault rifle. She also had a wicked looking combat knife, a few grenades, and lots of magazines of ammo.

She reminded him of Akila.

And with the next thing she said, she reminded him even more of Akila.

"I'm going after Vanessa," she said. "This is exactly the kind of war that the two of us excel at. We're going to hit them hard and fast, keep them off-balance, soften them up. You can come find us when you put together a plan to deal with them. Until then, I'm going to fucking kill as many of these sick fucks as I can."

"Wait," David said. She sighed but held her place. He walked over to her. "I need to tell you the plan, so if you find wounded or the less battle-ready of us, you can send them to safety."

"Tell me," she said.

He whispered the plan hastily in her ear.

She grinned when he was done. "That's clever, David." She gave him a kiss suddenly, a hard one on the mouth. "Don't die out there, it's been too long since we've fucked."

"Right back at you. Good luck," he replied.

"Yep. You too." She paused. "One more thing: spray-paint yourself a different color, David. I nearly blew your head off."

And then she was done.

"Let's go," David said.

He set off at a brisk pace, leading Evie, April, Donald, Janice, Peter, and Amanda into the darkness of the woods, away from the brightly lit hospital and the bloody scene of death. They'd stripped the Marauder corpses of anything useful and now they were all armed, though he had emphasized the need of stealth to them.

He was a little worried about Donald. He couldn't tell if the man had a concussion or was just in shock due to the attack. Katya seemed convinced he didn't have one, but she was also distracted.

At this point, she was more about putting the combat in combat medic than anything else.

And now she was gone.

David regained his focus as he led them through the dark trees again, roughly tracing the route he'd taken. There was one thing he intended to do before getting to the first leg of the annoying journey he was going to have to take. He thought it was a good one though, and was once more glad that he and Ellie and Lara had thought ahead over the summer and taken on a number of little projects like this. This shit was going to save lives.

But he couldn't help but feel a little dwarfed and, if he was being honest, somewhat hopeless about the situation.

There had to be hundreds of them, maybe as many as five hundred of these assholes roaming all over the region.

Shit, for all he knew there could be a thousand of them.

He had no idea of enemy strength beyond 'powerful'. Enough to take over potentially five different settlements of varying sizes.

This was all such a fucking mess.

But David didn't let himself get bogged down in despair. It wouldn't serve him at all. Either he was going to be able to make good on his promise to those shitheads back there, or he was going to die. Because he *wasn't* going to live as a prisoner, nor was he going to allow anyone he knew to. He'd meant every word back there.

Okay, well…

Maybe he'd been lying about letting them go.

But he had the impression that these bastards would never willingly leave this place. Which made this whole thing a lot easier, at least. They were an evil, invading force, and he was going to murder every fucking last one of them.

"Wait," he whispered as they passed by the bunker again.

"What's wrong?" April asked fearfully.

"Nothing, just wait," he replied, and crouched by one of the bodies.

A moment later, he found what he was looking for: the abandoned radio. He checked it over quickly, it still seemed to be in working order. He turned the volume down as far as it would go without actually being turned off, then clipped it to his vest.

"Okay, let's go."

They set off again, hurrying across the clearing, heading east and back into the woods.

David had taken his silenced pistol back from April. He wished they had more silencers on them, like even a single other one, but they were hard to come by nowadays. Yet another thing he should have focused more on but he'd spent too much time slacking off.

Well, that wasn't true, he supposed. He'd worked his ass off and he couldn't think of fucking *every* contingency. David began leading them to the northeast as they moved through the trees. It was going to be dangerous, this plan of his, but it shouldn't be *too* dangerous.

No more dangerous than walking the woods at night, anyway.

The whole time, he kept his ears open for both the radio and their surroundings. Marauders weren't the only bad things out among the trees. A few times he had to freeze, as he thought he'd heard something or seen something in the woods with them, but only once did it turn out to be something. He froze as they neared the place he was looking for, convinced he'd seen something shift to his left. Pistol in hand, he waited and watched.

Clouds scudded over the moon, casting deeper shadows across the area. He tensed, sure that he had seen something.

Suddenly, he caught a glint directly ahead of him, maybe ten feet away.

In a split second he realized what he was seeing, aimed, and fired off two silenced shots. Something grunted in a raspy voice and slumped. He released the breath he'd been holding as the moonlight came back, the clouds gone.

A stalker lay dead among the trees and scrub brushes.

"How the fuck did you see that?" April whispered harshly.

"The light glinting off its eyes, come on," he replied.

They kept walking until he made them stop again, this time just beyond the treeline. Directly ahead of them and to either side was the vast expanse of the valley where the abandoned construction site lay, as well as the entrance to the tunnel system.

"Everyone be *really* careful," he said. "We're right at the edge of a huge drop. We're going to go down the road that leads into the valley, understand?"

He made sure they all responded and were paying attention, then he led them out of the forest and to the path that led down into the valley.

"David, we're going to stash people in the mines?" Evie whispered.

"No," he replied. "Trust me. I've got a plan. We *are* going through them, but that's not our final destination."

"Where then? We blocked all the entrances."

"I know. I'll explain the plan once we're inside, okay?"

"All right."

They made their way down the incline, then along the valley wall, heading back in the opposite direction when they reached the bottom, and ultimately managed to hit the entrance to the mining tunnels without running into anymore problems.

David felt a shiver of anticipation and, admittedly, fear ripple through him as he came to stand before the huge opening. The first time he'd come here and gone inside, it had been...*extremely* intense. It had been a long, miserable, harrowing day of clearing out tunnel after cavern after cave of stalkers. Just...stalkers. Everywhere. But, in the end, they had triumphed.

They'd triumph again.

He and some of the others had taken to patrolling it periodically, just in case the stalkers decided to try and turn it into a nesting ground again. First every two weeks, then every three weeks, finally once a month. In all that time, they'd only run into a handful of hostiles down there.

The occasional stalker or ripper that had wandered in, nothing more. No evidence that any of them had gained a foothold since the initial extermination. It had been about a month since the last time he'd been here. He hoped it was still safe.

"What are we doing here?" April asked uncertainly.

David turned on his flashlight and aimed it in. "Inside first," he replied.

CHAPTER FOUR

They walked about thirty feet into the initial tunnel and he played his light across the way ahead and any nearby openings. It seemed clear, and he didn't smell the particular stink of any of the undead lingering around.

"Flashlights on," he said.

He checked the radio again, then turned it off entirely. He hadn't heard a peep from it so far, which was odd. Why wasn't there any radio chatter? A mystery for later. He turned to regard the group of tired, haggard people.

"Okay, here's the plan. Last month, Ellie and Akila and Ashley and I came back here and performed a sweep of the tunnels, like usual. This time, however, Ellie had a smart idea: she wanted to use these tunnels as a potential escape route. We managed to find a section of one tunnel that was just a few feet from the surface. We spent the day digging it out and reinforcing it with some metal we found in the tunnels. It lets out beyond the factory, by the lake. That's where we're going."

"What's back there?" Janice asked uncertainly. "Why is it safe?"

"There's a woman who lives by herself on the far side of the lake. We know each other and she's a friend."

"You want us all to go to Helen's house?" Evie asked.

He shook his head. "No. *The island.*"

Evie's eyes widened. "Holy shit, that's a good idea," she whispered.

"What if they're already there?" Peter asked

quietly.

"There's no one on the island normally. Hopefully they'll either not bother with it, or they'll have already gone to it and found nothing but trouble and gone back. There isn't practically anything beyond the lake, not for a long way, just Helen's house, and it's mostly hidden from view by trees and the island itself. I'm betting we might be able to figure out a way to get to the island from the back. We can get a little base of operations going there. I can pass people through this tunnel, to her house, to the island. That can be our fortress."

"It's dangerous," Janice muttered, then sighed softly. "But everything else is more dangerous. It *is* a good idea," she conceded.

"Exactly. So let's go. I want to get there as fast as possible."

They set off.

Before, it had taken David and the group about an hour to get to where they were going in the mines, but they hadn't exactly been hurrying. He figured that if they were quick and didn't run into any trouble, they might be able to get through the darkness in twenty minutes.

Of course, his plan relied on a lot of things. The opening still being open. There being no Marauders around, or undead, or few enough of them to deal with quickly. Helen being home, and amenable to the plan. There being boats to get to the island.

It would take luck and skill.

But mostly luck.

Nobody spoke as they made their way through the darkness. The air was still and dank, smelling of raw earth and old blood and older metal. They checked down every dark opening or side passageway as they approached it, wary of any undead or even Marauders that might be lurking down here. They seemed to have done their homework on the region, which bothered him.

A few things were bothering him. The primary one being: how the fuck did they know about him and Evie? They had identified and specified them as persons of interest. After ruminating on it for a bit, he supposed they could have interrogated anyone they had captured and gotten to know the leadership of Haven. Most people wouldn't break, but they weren't all hardasses.

They also could have been doing reconnaissance for days before the actual assault. They seemed well-trained and focused, to a certain degree.

Now there was a creepy thought: these fuckers watching him through binoculars from afar while he worked or hell, even fucked or slept. Though usually he did that behind closed doors. Speaking of fucking...

He glanced at Evie, then at April.

He actually *really* wanted to have sex all of a sudden. It was surprising how intense the lust hitting him presently was. Was it because he'd been comatose for two days? David couldn't remember the last time he'd gone a full twenty four hours without sex at least once. Shit, he couldn't remember the last whole day he'd gone without it twice.

No, he thought, maybe it had to do with the new level of threat he found himself under. There was probably some kind of correlation between life-threatening madness and lust.

No. Focus. Time was of the essence.

They made it most of the way there before something happened. David froze abruptly about twenty meters shy of the exit they'd made. He held up his fist in the light and everyone froze behind him. All became still. He waited, listened. Suddenly, he turned right, towards one of the offshoot tunnels, and shined his light down it.

Half a dozen figures appeared.

Stalkers. They were low to the rocky ground, in the process of slinking through the dark towards the fresh meat that had wandered into their lair. David cursed and opened fire with his submachine gun. The others joined in, several pistols popping off, the sound painful in the tunnel. He hoped they were far enough away from any Marauders and deep enough underground that the sound wouldn't be a factor.

The stalkers shrieked and ran into the gunfire, trying to dodge around it, trying to get at them with the single-minded determination only a monster could have. David splattered their old blood across the earthen walls as he emptied the magazine into them. As he hastily reloaded, he heard more wild shrieking coming from the other direction.

Spinning around, he just barely managed to get the freshly reloaded SMG up in time to send a burst of gunfire into the inhuman mask of a face he saw sprinting dead for him. The spray of bullets tore away most of its skull, splattering its rotting brains across more behind it.

Gritting his teeth, David continued hosing them down, running through an entire second magazine and punching bloody holes in their bodies. The second wave of stalkers was put down as the others finished up with the first and joined him in his firefight.

As he reloaded again, he stopped and listened, trying to slow his breathing and his pulse back down. He didn't hear anything.

"Fuck," he whispered. "Okay, let's go. Quick and quiet."

They continued making their way down the mining tunnel, moving towards its end, stepping over the corpses they'd just created. The path, at least, was pretty simple. Technically, there was just one fork in the main tunnel where it wasn't necessarily clear which way 'forward' was. But the good news about that was that if you forgot or didn't know, and chose wrong, it terminated after about a hundred feet in a dead-end, and you could just go back and go down the other one.

Of course, now it was obvious that there were stalkers down here. But he doubted there were many more lurking around, they would've come running at the sound of the battle.

Up ahead, he saw moonlight.

"We're almost there," he said. "Flashlights off."

Everyone turned off their flashlights and they moved more carefully the last thirty feet or so. David had them wait about ten feet away from the hole itself. They'd created it right where the roof met the end of the tunnel, so there had been a nice place to put a ladder they'd found in the trailers. It was metal and pretty sturdy. He'd wedged it pretty firmly into place.

"Stay here," he said, and mounted the ladder.

Letting his SMG dangle from its sling, he climbed up the metal rungs, looking up through the opening. All he could see was sky and dim moonlight. All he could hear was the occasional gust of wind and the sound of insects quietly chirping or buzzing or humming. Well, no way to find out but to stick his head up.

David climbed until he stood on top of the ladder

and stuck his head up.

He looked around, doing a complete three sixty carefully, scanning the whole area. In the distance, behind him, he saw the dark bulk of the abandoned factory. He could just make out some lights beyond it and farther to the right: the fishing village. There were no gunshots coming from that direction, and it was too far away to see anything more than the lights themselves. Well, *someone* was there, at least.

There was nothing to his left or right, and the way ahead looked clear, too.

"Okay, come on up. Evie, you next. Be careful," he said.

The ladder was sturdy, but she weighed the most of any of them. He was glad that he and the others had taken the time to make the hole big enough for a goliath. He pulled himself completely out of the hole and crouched by it, continuing to keep a lookout as Evie came up after him.

When she emerged from the hole, he helped her out, then he continued standing guard while she took over the duty of helping the others out. After about five minutes, they were all up and out of the hole. David felt impatient by now.

"Let's go," he said, whispering. "Stay close to me. Do *not* lag behind, do *not* lose focus. It's easy to get lost out here."

The light they'd had before from the moon had diminished by half, as some cloud cover had settled in over it. David kept his silenced pistol in hand as he made his way west and slightly south, towards the lake. They had to hit its corner and go around. As he looked at the vast expanse of the lake, just visible in the dim light, he suddenly remembered Azure. Shit! She could help! Her and her clan, maybe, but definitely her.

She would be a tremendous ally. She had been quite capable.

He made a note to either get someone to go upriver and enlist her help, or do it himself at some point. Maybe when day came he'd deal with it. David put it out of his mind for now. In this moment, all that mattered was reaching Helen's house. He couldn't see any lights at all coming from that direction and even though he knew her house was at least partially obscured by trees, he couldn't help but worry.

David found his mind trying, very hard, to turn towards Cait.

Fuck did he wish he could just go to her right this very second, just sprint in a straight line directly to her and just *see* her, and shoot any motherfucking Marauder he saw. He tried to stay focused as they hit the lake and began moving along its edge, towards Helen's house, but it was so difficult.

In a way, he still felt very guilty about how hung up on Cait he was, though he at least had more of an excuse now: he had Evie and April with him. He *knew* they were safe and sound for a fact. He could just look back at them.

But not Cait.

And there was more to it. She was pregnant with his child. Seven goddamned months pregnant. He *had* to find her, and soon. But wherever she was, if she was still alive–

No. No.

She was alive. He felt positive of that.

He *had* to believe that.

But wherever she was, it was almost certainly somewhere heavily guarded. These people were looking for local leaders, and she was definitely a local leader. It was possible that she'd gotten out, but he didn't like her odds. Then again, it had been a damned miracle that he'd managed to make it out of there alive and intact, thanks to Evie. Shit, there was so much to do! People to find, Marauders to kill, places to visit, plans to enact...

David clenched his jaw and then bit his tongue. Not enough to draw blood, but enough to get his ass to fucking *focus* again.

If he was going to somehow pull this whole thing off, he was going to need a razor focus, and he was going to have to go for days.

Finally, after what felt like far too long, they approached Helen's house. Still no lights on, but maybe she'd got clued into what was happening. She must have. And she was a sharp woman. He half-expected her to call out into the darkness that she had them covered with a sniper rifle and to identify themselves. But they got up to the house and then onto the front porch without hearing so much as a peep.

David knocked on the door. "Helen, it's David...are you in there?" he asked.

He waited. A few seconds went by. He knocked harder. Shit, if she was dead or gone, that would make this more difficult. Though they could still use her house as a staging area to stash people temporarily between the mines and the island.

Right as he resolved to just break in, the door suddenly opened up and he found himself staring down the wide bore of a shotgun.

"H-Helen," he managed, not even sure if it was her on the other end of that shotgun. It lowered suddenly and her middle-aged, rough, attractive face came into view.

"David, fuck. It's good to see you," she said, sounding genuinely relieved. She looked back over his shoulder. "Shit, you've brought a convention to my damned house."

"I'm sorry, but we need your help. Desperately," he replied.

She sighed, then grunted and stepped back. "Come on, get in here. Hurry up."

"Let's go," David hissed, waving them in.

He kept watch, making sure they didn't have any tails trailing after them, as the group hurried inside. But he didn't see anything, and once they were all inside, he followed and shut the door behind him.

"Do you know what's happening?" he asked as he stepped up to Helen.

"Not really," she replied. "A bunch of shitheads in dark clothes showed up and took over. That's all I've been able to determine. I've been watching from a distance with binoculars for a while. I heard the firefights two nights ago and assumed the worst. It's good to see you all."

"You too," he replied. "That's basically the gist of it. They call themselves Marauders. They're a very large, organized group of assholes who believe might makes right, it seems. I was knocked out during the initial invasion and just woke up a few hours ago."

"Damn," Helen muttered. "You doing okay?"

"I'm fine," he replied, although his head was hurting again and his body ached from pushing himself so hard after waking up from a two-day nap. "But listen, I need your help."

"What do you need?" she asked, sounding only mildly reluctant. She'd been fairly distrusting of him when he'd first come to her, seeking out the squid clan. Although he could tell she'd definitely grown to like him given their several sexual encounters since then.

"I need a place I can safely stash wounded and civilians," he replied. "I was thinking the island. Do you think you can find some boats and get to and from the island on this side of the lake without being discovered?"

Her frown deepened and she looked down at the floor for a moment. She didn't say anything for a full minute, then looked back up.

"It's possible," she said finally. "I know where we can rustle up a few boats. I see what you're getting at. You get people to my house, and when it's safe, I get people to the island on the boats. What if they're already on the island?"

"I'm sending along a few people who know how to fight. And, I mean, at this point we *all* know how to fight in an emergency," David said. "None of us are completely defenseless. But unfortunately these are the cards we've been dealt, so I'm playing them."

"Okay. Yes, I'll make this happen. Who's staying to help me?" she asked.

"Everyone but me," David replied.

None of the hospital staff argued, and although April looked anxious, she also seemed somewhat relieved. There was no way he was bringing her back out there. He looked at Evie, who seemed a bit torn as she met his gaze.

"I need you here, to help oversee this, honey," he said, stepping up to her.

"I know, I know. It makes the most sense. It's just...you're going back out there. There's hundreds of people out there looking to capture or kill you," she replied.

"I know, but our friends need my help. I have to

get back into the fight, faster the better, since I can move most freely at night."

"Yeah...just...don't do anything stupid," she said after a moment.

He laughed. "I can't really promise that."

She sighed and hugged him to her. "Just come back to me alive."

"I promise I'll try my absolute fucking best to do that. I have no intention of dying out there," he replied, hugging her back. "Do you know where to set up a basecamp?" he asked.

"I've been thinking about that since you first told me the plan. If I recall correctly, there was an abandoned hotel not far from the shore on the southwest corner of the island. And we could land the boats not too far from it."

"Good plan," he said. "See, you're a natural at this. You'll be a fine leader."

"I'll keep them safe, David," she replied. "And we've got most of the doctors with us. They'll be able to help fix any wounded you send our way."

"Exactly," he said. David let go of her and considered his next action. He needed to get back out there. But his head was throbbing and he was starving. He needed a short break. Just a very short one. "Come here for a minute."

Evie followed him over to April, who was still standing not far from the door, looking anxious still. He took her hand and led them both into the kitchen.

"This might be the last time we get to see each other for a while," he said as he shrugged out of his pack and set it on the table. He began rummaging around in it. "So I thought we should take the opportunity to spend a little bit of time together. I need to eat before I go."

"I could eat," April murmured, and Evie nodded.

April didn't have a pack on her, so he and Evie passed her a tin of shredded beef. David sat down at the table with his canteen, a tin of tuna, and a can of peaches, and consumed his meal. For a few moments, none of them spoke, merely eating.

When he was finished, he looked over at April. "How are you holding up?"

"I'm scared," she replied, then laughed morosely. "Really scared."

"I know, but you're doing so well, babe. You've come *so* far. You're so brave now."

She frowned and hugged herself suddenly. "I don't *feel* brave."

"Most people don't," Evie replied. "Bravery isn't a feeling so much as it is acting regardless of your feelings. You've been very brave."

"Thanks," she murmured. Then she looked at them. "It is going to be okay? I mean, are we *really* going to be okay? We've worked so fucking hard over the last several months, done so many great things, fought off so many threats, and now these fucking assholes just roll in and take everything over. We can...we can *do* this, right?"

"Yes," David replied firmly. "Believe me, I'm not letting this go. I know for a fact Ellie and Akila and Katya and Vanessa and Lara will *never* let something like this go, and they'll never cut and run. I think almost none of us will. There's too much invested in making this place our own. And now we've got Val and Lori's whole group. Val by herself is an absolutely brutal badass. Trust me, they're going to break on us like fucking water on a rock. They caught us by surprise but they are absolutely *fucked,* they're *dead,* they just don't know it yet."

David heard something behind him and looked over. He saw that everyone, all the personnel from the hospital and Helen, had gathered in the doorway to the kitchen.

"What? What's wrong?" he asked.

"We're listening to you," Helen replied. "You sound pretty motivated."

"I am. Don't worry, the Marauders are fucked. Between the likes me and Ellie, Lara and Jennifer, Akila and Azure, Lima Company, Val and her people, Katya and Vanessa, Ashley, all the other badasses we've seen among our people, we're going to wipe them out. Utterly."

"Can't say you lack for confidence," Donald murmured. "I hope you're right."

"You just make sure you stitch up whoever we send your way, and keep that island safe," David replied.

"We will," Janice replied.

David turned back to the remains of his meal. He tossed the last peach half into his mouth, drained the rest of his canteen, and then stood up. "I have to go now. Can I get a refill?" he asked, looking at Helen.

"Yeah, give it here," she replied.

He handed her the canteen and she went deeper into the kitchen. A moment later she returned with it topped off with fresh water. He secured it in his pack, took one last look over his arsenal, then he gave Evie and April a long kiss and a longer hug. Telling them that he loved them, and promising he'd come back safe, he began to head for the door.

"Hey, where's my sugar?" Helen asked.

He looked back at her, then chuckled awkwardly and moved over to her. "Sorry."

"Yeah, yeah," she replied, and kissed him on the

mouth. "Don't forget it's been too long since our last 'meeting'. When this is over..."

"It's a date," he replied.

He wished everyone good luck, then headed back out into the night.

...

"I knew it!" David whispered softly to himself.

He'd managed to make it back to the hole in the ground and through the mines without a problem. Not only that, but, as he retraced his route, he found that he could move a hell of a lot faster by himself. He suddenly had much more sympathy for Akila and Katya. No wonder they'd gone off by themselves. It was so much easier to do things when you didn't have to watch out for other people. Although that couldn't last forever.

As soon as he'd emerged from the mining tunnels, he'd made his way over to the pair of trailers by the abandoned construction site. He'd been thinking about what Katya had told him, about his uniform. She was right, he needed to find a different color or someone was going to wind up shooting him on accident.

And when he'd thought about it, something had nagged at him. It grew more powerful the closer he drew back to the construction site. Finally, he'd had it: he could have sworn he remembered seeing spray-paint cans around this area. So he'd made his way over to the trailers in search of those elusive items.

The first trailer had yielded nothing, and he'd almost given up his search on the second one, but finally, at the back, among some trash, he'd found one can. It was a flat gray color and it was almost full.

He looked around for a moment, considering it, then ended up moving back outside. He moved over to the half-constructed building, crouched among its shadowed interior, and took off the top half of his tactical outfit.

Making sure the gear attached to it was off or hidden within the pockets securely, he adjusted the nozzle where the paint would come out to the widest variant and quickly applied a layer of paint to the gear after shaking the can. The job was oddly calming, though he did feel the press of time and didn't linger. He coated his gear in the simple gray paint and once he was finished, pulled it all back on, made sure everything was where it was supposed to be, then stood and headed back out of the abandoned building.

Now...he had a job to do.

CHAPTER FIVE

David found that he was having trouble focusing.

A lot of trouble. The further he crept through the dark forest, the more he had to fight the urge to turn back around and run in a straight line towards the new settlement, where he was almost positive Cait was.

He'd passed almost within visual range of it not that long ago.

It was becoming very difficult not to go back and kill every fucker in dark armor there. But now wasn't the time, he'd just go and get himself captured or killed, and even in his rage and terror he could see that. So he'd soldiered on.

After the spray-painting job, he'd made a beeline for the nearest cache, in the watchtower north of the hospital. It was obvious that someone had been through, he hoped Vanessa, as several weapons were missing. But there was enough left that he'd filled his pack with some more rations and medical supplies, and a bit more ammo. From there, he'd immediately started making for another cache, one he thought he might possibly find either a person at or around, or maybe a note. It was the watchtower he'd first fucked Ellie in.

Fuck, what he wouldn't give to have her with him right now. He was making excellent time by himself, but having her with him would be comforting in a number of ways. David shook his head, trying again to regain his focus. He kept trying to generate more of a plan, but at the moment he didn't really have one.

He felt switched on, but like he was just spinning his wheels in place. There didn't seem to be much more beyond 'find more guns and ammo, kill more Marauders'. Again, he had a great deal of sympathy for Ellie and Akila and Katya.

David froze as he heard a voice from up ahead. He switched to his pistol and began to slowly make his way forward again. There was another voice, two of them, both unfamiliar. And then he saw lights in the darkness.

Coming from the direction of the watchtower he was heading for. Well, shit. Could be good or bad but he figured it would be bad. Maybe it was high time he started making good on that payback he owed the Marauders, though. David continued creeping forward through the underbrush.

He began to make out voices.

"Just come down from there and we won't hurt you," someone was saying. Shit, they had someone trapped up in the watchtower. "We've got orders to bring you in."

"Fuck off!" a familiar female voice snapped, and a wild gunshot was fired.

Several curses followed.

"What the fuck are we gonna do?" someone muttered, just barely loud enough for David to hear now that he was closer.

"We'll figure something out," another voice replied.

David carefully replaced his silenced pistol. No need for stealth at this point, if anyone was around they already knew gunfire was to be expected. He grabbed his SMG and shifted slowly into position, peering through the vegetation into the clearing the watchtower was built in.

There were seven of them. Great. He couldn't see any others around and three were pointing flashlights up. Four of them were clustered together right in front of David, with two others off to the right and another one by themselves off to the left.

Fine then, it was time to kill.

He got carefully into position, took aim, and let loose. The submachine gun roared in his grasp and the bullets immediately began chewing into the backs of the unsuspecting Marauders. He hosed them down, emptying the whole magazine into them. The surviving three began to run away while also twisting around, weapons drawn, but whoever was up top, (he recognized that voice suddenly, Ashley, it was Ashley up there), popped up and opened fire. She shot the one to the left in the head and then twisted to fire on the other two. David let his SMG drop and hang as it ran dry, then whipped out his pistol and opened fire on the two runners.

He and Ashley gunned them down fast.

"Who the fuck's down there?" Ashley asked, now aiming in his general direction.

"Ashley, it's David," he replied.

"Oh fuck, thank God," she replied. "I'm coming down."

"No, stay up there, keep watch. I'll be up in a second," he said.

"Okay. Hurry."

She sounded in control, but the fear and stress were obvious in her voice. He quickly moved among the dead, checking them over with his pistol in hand, ready to put them out of their misery if they were still alive. No one in the central group was, nor was the woman who'd been off by herself.

But he found a single survivor among the two they'd both gunned down. A pale man with a lot of muscles on him. Several bullets had penetrated him, as blood was leaking out of holes in his chest armor, and some was coming out of his mouth.

He coughed as David kicked away a gun.

"You aren't gonna win," he grunted, wheezing as he stared up at David. "Everyone always fights. People don't win."

"Who the fuck are you? What the hell do you want?" David growled.

"We're the Marauders–"

"Yeah, yeah. I got that already. Obviously you're here as an occupying force, but what's your fucking goal?"

"You're all going to be inducted into the Marauder ranks. All of you will serve or die. We're going to break you," he growled, then broke into a coughing fit. "There is no third option."

"What, do you honestly believe your little army has won every single battle it's ever fought?" he asked.

"Of course!" he snarled. "We are strength against the weakness. We will cull the weakness from your ranks and bring the strong into our own."

"No you won't," David replied.

He aimed the pistol and fired a shot into the man's forehead. Immediately his body went slack as his brains were splattered across the dirt. David stared at the body for a second, then shook his head and hurried over to the watchtower as he reloaded his weapons. He found Ashley standing at the top of it, waiting for him.

She immediately wrapped him in a hug.

"Where have you been!?" she whispered harshly as she squeezed him against her.

"I can tell I'm gonna get tired of answering this," he muttered. "Comatose for two days. Just woke up a few hours ago."

"Have you seen anyone else?" she asked.

"Yes. Inside. Let's gather some supplies while we talk. I imagine that's why you were here?" he asked as they went into the single room at the top.

"Yeah," she replied. "I was on my way to the farmers, to see if they might be able to offer some kind of help. I don't really know what's up with them," she replied.

"I heard they're under control of the Marauders," he said as he started sifting through the supplies, finding the best material and leaving most of the rest for anyone else who came this way. "Have you seen anyone else?" he asked.

"Yes. I ran into Val and Lori," she replied. "They were by the river. They managed to get away. I guess the Marauders were taking them and some others over to the outpost at the hunting grounds, not sure why though. Val and Lori managed to get away when a pack of stalkers attacked the group. That was earlier today. They'd been on the hunt for people to help them take down the Marauders that are at the hunting grounds. They want to rescue the people there."

"Did they have any success?" he asked.

She sighed. "No, so far I was the only one they'd found. They told me to meet them at a spot near the hunting lodge about an hour and a half from now with anyone I could find and whatever guns and ammo and supplies I could get my hands on. I thought I'd swing by here and then see if I could convince the farmers to help..."

"Why them? They've always sat out," David replied.

"I know but they're the only ones I wasn't completely sure about. Everyone else has been taken over. I saw the fishing village, it's all taken over. Shot up, too, so they put up a fight. But it's definitely taken over now."

"Wait, what about Lima Company?" he asked.

She sighed. "I haven't seen them, but I overheard some of the Marauders talking. They said 'the Marines were neutralized' before this even started apparently."

"Great," he muttered. "What happened to you?"

She sighed and shook her head. "Ellie got me out when it became obvious we were fucked. We spent that night hunting and most of the first day hiding, ambushing occasionally. She...was losing it. Going fucking crazy with rage and anger. She was scaring me. Finally, we got to a cabin in the middle of nowhere last night and she told me to just stay put. She'd sort this out. I begged her not to go alone, but she did and I haven't her since."

"Evie saw her at some point, but that's what she said, that she was almost feral. God, I hope she's okay. I saw Akila earlier. She was fine but basically doing the same thing: hunting. But listen, I've got some good news at least. Evie, April, Helen, and everyone from the hospital but Katya and Vanessa are safe and sound across the lake.

"They're going to get to the island and start setting up a basecamp, away from the Marauders, and we're going to get people to them to get them to safety. I saw Katya but she did the same damn thing: headed off on her own with murderous intent. Vanessa's somewhere out there doing the same already, last I heard. But listen, I need to tell you the plan to get people to safety if we get separated."

"I'm listening," she replied, looking over at him intently. He quickly explained it to her and she began nodding before long. "Okay, yeah, that makes sense. Man, I'm glad we dug that hole. It's going to be *so* damned helpful."

"Yep. Now, let's go see what the situation is with the farmers. Maybe we can talk to someone on the down low. But either way, after that, we go straight to the meeting area. I don't know if the four of us are going to be enough to mount an assault, but it might be if three of those people are you, me, and Val."

"I'm good to go," she said as she zipped her pack up and slipped it back on.

He looked her up and down. She was wearing brown and green clothing, like something Ellie would wear: tanktop, cargo pants ripped off at the knee, boots. Her hair was tucked up into a beanie, her face dirty, her eyes tired but determined. She had a combat knife on her thigh, a pistol on her hip, and her pockets bulged with ammo.

"Let's get you properly armed," he said, and they began heading back down to the corpses they'd made not too long ago.

...

They salvaged the guns and ammo from the dead Marauders, taking the excess and storing it up in the watchtower.

When they went back up there a second time, he said, "You know this is where I first fucked Ellie? Right there in that bed. She was so weird about it."

Ashley laughed. "Really?"

"Yeah. She came onto me. Like she was mad that she was horny."

"That sounds like Ellie."

They finished storing the gear and then moved the bodies out of obvious sight. As they headed off again, he suddenly asked, "Does it weird you out at all? The way I talk about fucking Ellie? I can not bring it up if you don't like it."

"No, I don't care," she replied. "Although..." she sighed softly. "I still feel like whatever you and Ellie have is different than what me and Ellie has. Stronger. I don't know. I mean I've fucked you often enough too and I know we've got a nice bond going, just...it's a little off-putting. I guess I'd be worried about you stealing her from me if you weren't so obviously in love with Cait. And Evie and April," she explained.

He laughed. "I wouldn't do that. Come on."

"I don't think you'd do it on purpose, it's just...if it were a choice between you and me, I think she'd choose you."

"I think you might just be being paranoid," David replied, although he *did* wonder. Not that he wanted to come between the two women at all. He just wanted people to be happy. "She loves you," he said firmly. "That's what matters. She loves you."

"She loves you too," Ashley replied.

"I know, but what we have...it's different. But not in the way you might think." He sighed. "I don't know. Try not to worry about it. She loves you, you're her girlfriend, you love her. You're living together and you get along well enough. It's fine."

"Yeah I guess so," she muttered after a moment.

They fell silent as they walked on through the dark forest. David kept scanning the horizon, expecting to see the first hints of dawn appearing, but the skies were still dark. He couldn't know for sure, but he had an idea that dawn was somewhere within the next few hours. They didn't have a lot of time to play with.

Daylight was going to complicate things.

Ten minutes later, they reached the edge of the woods surrounding the farmhouses. He sighed softly as he studied what he saw. They had several lights on and he could clearly see the dark-suited forms of several Marauders within the fenced-in plot of land. As he sat there staring, however, he saw a lone figure at the back.

"Who is that?" Ashley whispered.

"I think..." He paused. Saw a sullen orange glow by the figure's face, which became more visible. It was Thatch, he realized. The man who ran the farms. He was smoking a pipe. "Holy shit. Wait here. Don't move, I'll be right back."

"Okay," Ashley replied uncertainly.

David took one last look around, then quickly slipped away into the darkness, towards the farmhouses. William Thatch stood near the back corner nearest David, out of the light mostly. This was risky. He might be discovered. But it seemed free of Marauders or other people, and even if Thatch had turned control over to them, he thought that the man wouldn't actually turn against him. Thatch had too much stubborn respect for him at this point, because of all he had done for not just his farms, but the region around them.

"Thatch," he whispered as he reached the edge of the well-made fence. William let out a soft gasp and nearly dropped his pipe. David could just see him in the moonlight now.

"W-who's there?" he whispered.

"David."

"Oh my God, I thought you were dead," he

muttered, drawing closer after checking over his shoulder. "What are you doing here?"

"Checking on you. What's happened? Obviously the Marauders have taken over your farms."

He sighed softly. "The morning after all the shooting, they came. Told us they were willing to offer us a deal: autonomy and exemption from enslavement for my people if I agreed to work with them and provide food and resources. I...agreed."

"Honestly, can't blame you," David muttered.

"What's happening out there? They won't tell us anything."

"It's bad. They control everything, but some good people are out and fighting. I'll spare you the details. Suffice to say, this isn't over by a damn sight. We're going to nail these bastards to the wall. Can you help at all?"

"Presently, no," William replied flatly. "It's too dangerous. But...if you manage to launch some coordinated assault, some final attack that you think can actually win, I will throw my lot in with yours. We'll arm and help."

"Good. You promise?" he asked.

"I promise. You have my word," he replied.

"I'll hold you to that, Thatch, and we'll come calling later. I promise that we're going to kick these bastards out of here. For now, keep your people safe. And ready."

"Understood. But I do have *one* bit of news for you," he said.

"What?" David asked, perking up. It'd be nice to come away from this with a *little* more.

"I heard them talking not too long ago. They said some people got away from Haven and they're tracking them. They mentioned something about the old burned down settlement. I think that's where your people got to."

"River View," David muttered. "Thanks."

"You're welcome. Good luck out there."

"You too."

David slipped off, hurrying back to rejoin Ashley.

"Well?" she asked.

"They're out of the game for right now. But we've got a new job."

"What's that?"

"We're going to try and rescue some people in River View."

...

"You're sure they're here?" Ashley whispered.

They weren't far from the broken wall where he and Evie had escaped over all those long, long months ago. He was feeling an intense emotional swelling in him as he looked at the wrecked ruins of the settlement. It had been months since he'd come back.

They'd returned a few times after winter to search it more thoroughly for supplies, but it had been dangerous. Mostly they just tracked down old items that had some value or personal meaning to those who had survived that brutal attack and the massive fire that it had caused.

"No," he replied. "But it's worth checking out."

He peered through the gap in the wall, which had collapsed more since that fateful night, and immediately saw movement.

"Marauders," he muttered, SMG at the ready.

"Well, at the very least we'll get to put some of

them down," she whispered.

"Come on, there's a bigger gap in the wall we can slip through over here."

They moved to the left, as silent as death, around the corner of the exterior wall that had once surrounded the settlement, and came to a larger gap. Okay, this was it. Another assault, another chance that he might not walk away. He studied the layout.

There weren't any on this end, where the street that ran the length of the settlement terminated in the crumbling wall. They were gathered near the center, the main junction a little ways away, apparently gathering to get orders. It looked eerily similar to how he had first met Ashley, in that very spot.

If she noticed the parallels, she didn't say anything.

"They're clustered kind of tightly together," he whispered. "We could take them out quick...if we get lucky."

"I'm ready when you are," she whispered.

"See that little tree there?" he asked, pointing down the length of the wall to the left.

She looked and nodded. "Yeah, I see it."

"If I remember right, there's another opening in that wall. It should give you a great view of them. Hurry up and get down there. I'll get closer. Open fire when I do."

"Got it. Good luck."

"You too."

They split up. He slipped in, grateful for the cover of night, and hurried over across the street. He passed by his old shack, hiding in the shadows. He listened as he drew closer and began to make out the sound of a man's deep voice.

"Okay, we know they're somewhere in here. This

is the group that managed to get away from Haven. Time has come to make an example. We're going to execute one of them as a sign to the others that they're beaten and they need to stop wasting time struggling, that they need to just give up, lay back, and let it happen. Now, find them. But just bring them to me, don't hurt them more than you have to. I want the execution to be very public."

Okay, wow, holy shit. He *really* needed to get to it.

David slipped up as close as he could. He'd counted a dozen of them. Taking aim with his SMG, he hoped for a repeat of last time. Just as he caught sight of Ashley on the other side of the wall, just barely visible only because he knew where to look and what to look for, he dug in and prepared to go to war.

There was an open door right beside him, so he could duck in there for cover if he needed to. Taking aim, he saw that they were beginning to disperse. Okay, this was really it. Now or never. He squeezed the trigger.

The SMG spoke in his grasp, rounds rattling out in an awful spray of metal death. He hosed the central core of the group down, holding the trigger down and firing until it was finished. He'd be using short, controlled bursts next time around. This time he just wanted shock and awe. Four of them went down and the rest began scattering.

Though even as he pulled back while reloading as the more cognizant of them returned fire his way, he saw the muzzle flare of Ashley's own weapon. They'd recovered another submachine gun from one of the Marauders they'd killed back at the watchtower and she was putting it to good use.

Another two went down under her gunfire. David felt a bullet nick his combat vest as he pulled back, getting into cover and hastily reloading. He had to keep the pressure up. As soon as he was reloaded, he leaned out, targeted one still in the open, and fired. A burst of bullets leaped out of his SMG and nailed him.

His armor seemed to stop two of them, but one punctured his neck and another got through his armor in an explosion of blood. He let out an awful gurgling sound as he staggered around, clutching at his throat.

David felt another round hit him, and this time it wasn't a graze. It felt like someone had punched him in the chest. He grunted, shifting behind cover, then blind-fired around the edge of the cover. Someone screamed. He heard Ashley popping off her own shots as he waited. *Damn* that had hurt!

He hoped it hadn't gotten through at all, but it was hard to tell. Ignoring the pain as best he could, David reloaded once more and then leaned carefully back around, ducking down lower this time. A bullet sailed by and then another smacked into the wall beside him, sending bits of brick everywhere. He saw the Marauder firing on him.

She was in between two structures. He took aim, hoping she didn't do to him what he was just about to try to do to her. Once she leaned out a little more to get a good aim on him, he squeezed the trigger again. The burst of bullets sent a few into her and she screamed and stumbled forward. A gunshot rang out from Ashley's position and a bullet smacked into the side of her head with a brutal efficiency. He quickly checked the bodies as he ducked back down, seeing if there were any survivors, but also how many they'd put down.

Ten. Ten were dead now. He then saw one of them shifting, rolling, and fired out another pair of shots to ensure that number remained correct. There were two more, at least. He leaned out and checked for more. He'd seen at least one of them scurry off down the road that turned the main road into a sideways T.

There was movement a bit farther down. David sighted them, then cursed as they slipped into a partially collapsed building. He slipped out around the corner and started making his way towards that person, trusting Ashley to watch his back. He managed to make it about twenty feet before he saw them again.

They were waiting for him. They saw him at the same moment he saw them and both of them aimed and fired. Another punch, this one to his gut, but the rest missed. His didn't. The barrage of bullets he released slammed into their chest and then one went right into the Marauder's mouth, killing him instantly as it severed his brain stem.

Now, where was that last–

David froze as he heard a metallic click behind him and felt the barrel of a gun being pressed to the back of his head. He started to spin while jerking his head to the side when he heard a gunshot go off.

He expected to die then, for some huge, unthinkable pain to erupt in his skull and then nothing, but the only thing that hurt were his ears, (and his head, too, still had that fucking headache), and there was a lot of warm liquid all over the back of his neck suddenly. He twisted around, bringing up his SMG, and saw a familiar face staring at him, holding a smoking pistol, a now dead Marauder crumpled in a heap between the two of them.

"Amanda, you saved my life," he said softly.

"Holy shit, it's good to see you," she replied, lowering the gun. "Are there any more?"

"I think that was the last one," he replied. "Stay here, let us sweep the area."

"Us?"

"Ashley is with me."

"Oh thank God," she whispered. "Hurry."

"I will, but get whoever's with you ready to go. We're working on a time limit, got it?"

"Got it," she replied, nodding tightly, then she disappeared back into the building. Damn it was good to see her. He whistled for Ashley to come out, and kept an eye out for more Marauders as she hurried to join him.

"What's happening? I saw you talking with someone," she asked.

"It was Amanda. There's others inside, but I don't know who. She's prepping them to move. Let's do a quick sweep of the area and make sure no one else is lurking, then we gather whatever supplies we can from the dead to send with Amanda and her group."

"Got it," Ashley replied.

They set to work, checking the most obvious areas for signs of life. They checked the broken windows and smashed in doors, the dark alleyways, using their flashlights at this point, but they found no one. Once they were reasonably sure they were clear, the pair began hastily gathering up whatever guns, ammo, and supplies they could find among the dead. A few minutes went by in the chilled silence. As he did his search, it really occurred to David that it was almost a bit chilly now. He glanced up, that cloud cover hadn't moved.

It would probably rain tomorrow, probably a misty curtain that would cover everything in a sullen sheen. Just another thing to add to the list. He loved rain, but he didn't so much like fighting for his life in it. By the time they were just about done collecting up the surplus from the latest batch of Marauder corpses, Amanda returned with a small group of people. He studied them in the glare the flashlights provided. Amanda seemed to be the leader. Her husband and daughter were there, as was Ben, the teenager they'd basically adopted. Besides them, there were three others. One he somewhat recognized as one of Val's people.

The last two were Chloe and Lena, the couple they'd rescued from the thieves back during winter who had ultimately decided to stay with them and tend the hydroponic garden with Jennifer. They all looked nervous and frightened.

"Is this everyone?" he asked.

"Yes," Amanda replied.

"Where's my family? Did you see them?" Ashley asked anxiously.

"As far as I know they're still back at Haven," Amanda replied. "They were still okay when I saw them last."

"Fuck," she muttered.

"I'm sorry, but we have to focus. Are any of you seriously injured? Can you all move quickly and quietly for a ways?" he asked.

Amanda conferred with everyone quickly, then turned back to him. "We're ready. Where are we going?" she asked.

"Somewhere safe, but we need to hurry. Grab everything we've gathered there and make sure you're armed," David replied, indicating the pile of excess weapons and supplies they'd placed on a nearby bench that had survived all the chaos.

The group quickly armed themselves and pocketed anything else that was there, then formed up before him and Ashley.

"All right. I want you all to be as quiet as possible. Stay with me, do *not* slow down and do *not* wander off. Speak up *only* if there's an emergency. Guns are an absolute last resort. There's way, way more of them than there are of us. Stay with me and Ashley, we're going to get you on the way to safety, understand?" he asked.

They all nodded to him.

"Okay...let's do this."

CHAPTER SIX

"You've got all that, Amanda?" he asked.

"Yes," Amanda replied firmly. "All the way down the main tunnel, right at the fork, out of the hole, around the back of the lake to Helen's house, and she'll get us to the island. Watch out for stalkers in the tunnels, and for everything else up top."

"Right," he said. "And *hurry*. Okay?"

"We will. Thank you so much, David," she replied, giving him a hug.

"Good luck," he said, hugging her briefly, then disengaging from her. "Evie will make sure you get to safety."

"Okay. Good luck to you," she said, then turned to the others. "Let's go, people."

David stood about twenty feet into the tunnel with Ashley and they spent a few seconds watching them go, hurrying away. They had sent off all the extra guns, ammo, food, and medical supplies they could possibly spare with the group, hoping it would be of more use for them and where they were going. Unwilling to wait any longer, David turned and began stalking away, out of the tunnel. Ashley followed after him.

"Where's this meeting place?" he asked, looking up as soon as they got back out. The skies were still dark.

"It's a clearing about a hundred yards west of the hunting lodge and cabins. The one with the hunter's blind, remember it?" she replied.

"I remember. Come on, we need to move faster," he replied, and began jogging towards the ramp that would take them out of the valley.

HAVEN 8

He didn't think of much during that jog, his mind
mercifully clear. In a way, it was almost like his fear
and guilt and anxiety over Cait and the others was an
infection, and rescuing Amanda and the others,
sending them off to safety, was like a shot of
antibiotics. It wasn't enough to cure the infection, but
it relieved the symptoms for a bit.

Saving people felt good, and he felt confident
Amanda was tough enough to get them to where they
were going. He noticed Ashley was very quiet and
focused too, but he imagined she was worried about
her parents, about her brother. He knew exactly how
she felt. But there was nothing they could do about
that now.

They ran up the ramp, the now chillier night air
actually pleasant with all the activity, then made their
way to the northern end of the land above the valley
and, as soon as they were able, immediately broke
east, heading by the valley's edge on that side and
then moving beyond the valley completely.

Although it probably took about half an hour to
make it there, it felt like they'd spent three hours
jogging through the dismal gloom.

But finally, his head clear, his mind focused,
David reached the edge of the clearing she had told
him about. He and Ashley crouched by it, waiting. He
looked out into the clearing beyond. There was
nothing there but a hunter's blind, a simple wooden
box raised a few feet off the ground by wooden struts.

He didn't see activity of any kind. The place
seemed totally deserted. He felt certain that they had
made it back within the hour and a half window, but
he had to admit that his timekeeping might not be
perfect.

"You sure this is the place?" he whispered.

"Yes," Ashley replied. She reached into her pocket and pulled out an old pocketwatch. "We synced watches. They should be here by now."

"Shit, that's useful," he muttered.

Then he turned his attention back to the clearing, scanning it carefully. He didn't see any uncertain lumps on the ground, nothing obvious among the trees that surrounded the clearing, and nothing around the hunter's blind itself. Although you could definitely duck down and hide inside of it, or maybe they were hiding on the other side of it. The moonlight only gave so much visual help.

"I'm going to go over there," he said. "Maybe they're inside."

"I don't know, something seems off," Ashley muttered.

David heard something behind him then and he spun around, SMG raised. He found himself staring down the barrel of a silenced submachine gun. The gun lowered suddenly and a familiar face appeared.

"Xenia," he whispered, trying to get his breath back. Fuck, he was going to age ten years over the next few days if this level of stress kept up.

"David. Ashley," the pale, petite woman replied.

She looked like an assassin, done up in jet black clothing, also wearing a black beanie like him, a pair of green goggles on her face. She looked very different from the first time he'd met her with Val and Lori's group in the quarry.

"What's up with those goggles?" he muttered, still off-kilter from having the woman scare the shit out of him. Ashley seemed to be trying to find her voice as well.

"Nightvision," she replied simply, and began checking over her SMG.

"Where in the hell did you get those?!" Ashley whispered harshly.

"Managed to kill someone important on the other side. They had some tactical gear on them. It's mine now. I've been using it against them," she replied. "I've been following you for a bit."

"I didn't hear you at all," he muttered.

"No, I'm very, very good at being quiet. But we have a problem. Val and Lori have been recaptured."

"Fuck..." David groaned, feeling the pit of his stomach drop out again.

"I have a plan," Xenia replied calmly.

"You have a plan that the three of us can enact to assault the hunting lodge and rescue everyone there?" Ashley asked uncertainly.

"Yes, but it's...risky. Unfortunately, we have no alternatives at the moment."

"What actually *happened* to Val and Lori?" he asked.

"They found me a little while ago. Or rather, I found them. Told me about the plan, about Ashley, and where to go. We were on our way here when we got jumped. Val told me to run and so I...did. There were a lot of them. Around thirty. I think they were going to back up the hunting lodge. Val took some of them out but they overwhelmed her and Lori and forced them to surrender. I was hidden up a tree and had a good view of them. They were taken back to the hunting lodge."

"Okay, I have a question," David said. "Why are you this like master of stealth? Are you a fucking assassin or something?"

She sighed. "Yes," she admitted. "Look, I don't have time to get into it right now. The plan is simple but...risky."

"Tell me," he said.

"I did some recon. There's a very large pack of stalkers lingering maybe a hundred yards away from the hunting lodge, on the other side. I want to rile them up, lure them to the lodge. In all the chaos, hopefully, the Marauders and stalkers will weaken each other, while the three of us also work to take them out where we can. Well, you two will do that, I'll be freeing and arming anyone I can to help even the numbers."

"That *is* very risky," Ashley murmured.

"Yeah, but she's right. We don't have a lot of alternatives and–" He looked down at the watch still in her hand. "What time is it?" he asked.

"I don't know, it wasn't telling the correct time when I found it so we turned it to midnight when we synced," she replied.

"Great," he muttered.

"It's about four in the morning," Xenia said. "Dawn is roughly two hours off."

"How do you know that?" Ashley asked.

"I'm good with timekeeping," she replied. "Can we do this?"

David sighed, considered it for a moment, really racked his brain to come up with some alternative, but based on everything he had here at the moment, he just didn't think there was another way out. Not unless they managed to find a big group of friendlies. But that wasn't going to happen.

Even if they managed to find Katya, Vanessa, Akila, and Ellie by some insane miracle...well maybe they could assault it that way, but it wasn't happening. So right now he saw no other way to deal with this than to use Xenia's insane plan.

He looked at her for a moment. He remembered

the first time he'd seen her, when he'd come to meet Val and Lori's group in the beginning. Even then, looking at her, he'd had a feeling about her. That this petite, pale woman, who he doubted broke five three and a hundred and ten pounds, was lethal. Dangerous. And he was completely right, apparently. He *needed* to learn more about her, but later. Another thing to throw onto the list of shit to do later.

"I'm ready," he said.

"Good. It should take me about ten minutes to get into position and rile them up. I'll run straight for the settlement, then slip in among the chaos. I already have a place picked out. You two hang back and pick off targets of opportunity from both sides. Don't want either side winning, obviously. And try to keep an eye out for friendlies," Xenia explained.

"Understood."

And then she was gone, racing off into the darkness, disappearing like a ghost.

"That woman scares me," Ashley whispered.

"Me too," he replied. "But she's our friend and we need to help her. So let's get to it."

...

The hunting lodge was lit up with several bonfires, and there was a lot of activity going on for the middle of the night.

As he and Ashley got into position, careful not to be seen by the outer perimeter guards, he couldn't help but think back to the winter assault on this place. He'd had a lot more people helping him and more idiotic opponents that time around.

Although he was becoming uncomfortable the more he thought about the strangely fanatic way in which the man he'd interrogated had gone on about the Marauders, almost like a cultist, he could tell they were a lot more organized. He'd taken down two groups so far, but he was getting lucky, and he knew it. And his luck might be wearing thin. He could feel those bruises the bullets had left.

That could have just as easily been his face.

Couldn't think about any of that now.

David instead found himself wishing he'd managed to get his hands on something a bit more long range, something with a damned scope, but it was out of the cards apparently. No, they were going to have to wait until the chaos started, then sprint up to the row of cabins that served as one of the walls, and shoot from there.

He was a good aim but he wasn't *that* damn good with a pistol in the dark at something like thirty meters. So they crouched there in the dark, not saying anything, moving as little as possible, and waited.

He glanced at Ashley. She looked ghostly and beautiful in the moonlight, and again he felt an intense spike of lust. He felt guilty, but Amanda had given him a look, that *fuck me hard* look. And that wasn't ego, he now knew for a *fact* that yes, that is what that look meant from her. Apparently he wasn't the only one who was having trouble controlling their libido. And even Ashley had glanced at him a few times with lust in her eyes so far.

What a shit time for lust and desire.

He turned away from her, before she looked over at him, noticed him staring, and either got annoyed or amused. Either way, it would distract them both and they couldn't afford that. Ashley checked her watch.

"Almost ten minutes," she whispered softly.

"I'm ready," David replied.

They kept waiting. After another moment, he thought he heard a distant gunshot. Then a second one. He tensed, ready to spring into action, and sensed Ashley doing the same beside him. He definitely heard a third gunshot, much louder, and suddenly several more followed. Someone fired a shotgun. Someone else blasted away with an assault rifle. People were shouting. And he began to hear a rising tide of stalker shrieks.

It was working.

As the guards on this side disappeared to help out, all but one of them, he saw, David and Ashley began sprinting. He took aim with his silenced pistol and capped the lone remaining guard, who stood atop one of the small cabins, with a clean headshot. Holstering the pistol again, he marveled at that. Holy shit, he'd just made a running headshot. He really *was* getting good at shooting. They hit the edge of the small settlement, really more of an outpost, and split up. He went in between two cabins, and she went in between two more off to the right.

David moved down the narrow alleyway, SMG at the ready, and saw chaos. Already, the stalkers were overrunning their outer defenses and he saw several moving among the buildings as the Marauders desperately tried to contain them. They were keeping calm, he gave them that, and killing the stalkers with a brisk proficiency.

If it weren't for him, Ashley, and Xenia, they would have been able to deal with this. Unfortunately, they were fucked. He aimed and fired a burst into the back of one Marauder who stood in front of him. The man went down under a flurry of bullets. David turned and sent a burst into another who had the high ground on another cabin across the way. One of the bullets caught him in the throat and he stumbled off, smashing into the ground where a pair of stalkers leaped onto him and savagely tore into him.

He kept up the fire, emptying his submachine gun as quickly as he could manage, putting down another five of the bastards before pulling back into the shadows to hastily reload. He could tell that the Marauders knew something was up, but they didn't seem to have pinpointed him or Ashley yet. Where was Xenia? He hadn't seen her so far. As he prepared to go in for another attack, he glanced up at the sound of shattering glass and saw a Marauder flying bodily through a window on the second story of the hunting lodge.

As the man screamed, falling through the air amid thousands of shards of broken glass, he briefly caught sight of a slight pale figure dressed in black in the frame of the broken window. How in the fuck had she gotten up there already?! Then she was gone. The body hit the ground with a solid thud. David resumed firing.

He saw scenes of utter chaos playing out before him. He saw a man trying to put down a trio of stalkers. He got one in the face, winged another, and then the third leaped onto him and knocked his gun from his hand.

The Marauder screamed as the two surviving stalkers began ripping into him. David almost felt bad. A trio of Marauders wielding shotguns were holding down a main entrance, blasting a wave of stalkers that were coming right for them. They were doing good, he saw. Really good. Two of them were always firing, allowing a third time to reload, firing in overlapping waves at alternating times.

They had a pile of dead stalkers before them.

Well, couldn't have that happening. David took aim and put a burst of bullets into the back of one of them. He flopped forward right as he began to raise his freshly reloaded shotgun, a bullet having taken him in the base of the neck. To their credit, the other two kept on firing.

But the stalkers almost immediately overran their position and they disappeared beneath a living, writhing wave of the inhuman monsters. David emptied the rest of his magazine into those stalkers. Couldn't have them getting *too* much of an upper hand now.

As he reloaded again, he saw the doors to one of the cabins literally explode open, flying off its hinges, and grinned fiercely as he saw the tall, muscular figure of Valerie come striding out with murder in her stride and death in her eyes. She located the nearest weapon, a shotgun, snatched it up off the ground, turned, and blew the nearest Marauder's head clean off.

Two more tried to respond to this sudden development but she pumped and fired two more times, blowing one's chest out and shooting a third man's arm off in a horrendous spray of blood. As she looked for more targets of opportunity, David saw a stalker coming at her.

He couldn't get a shot and he tried to shout a warning, but it was too noisy. Cursing, he left his hiding spot and fired off a burst. *That* got her attention. She swung his way as he put down the stalker, caught eyes with him briefly, then nodded tightly and went back to killing.

Hot damn it was good to see her out and about again.

There were more people he saw as he put down

another trio of stalkers and then reloaded hastily. More figures not wearing black. Friends. They were looking for weapons and, no doubt, opportunities to get some revenge. He couldn't look after them all, so he just focused on the area immediately around them.

It seemed like Xenia had gotten started on releasing the prisoners, though he couldn't see her at all. She could take care of herself. If any of them could, apparently it was her. As he put down another stalker that was leaping in from between a pair of cabins, he suddenly wondered who would win between Xenia, Ellie, and Akila.

Not the best thing to think about at the moment, but his mind was like quicksilver.

He emptied another magazine gunning down half a dozen stalkers and began making his way towards the main entrance they were coming through. Since he'd allowed them to overrun the main entrance, it seemed that a lot more had gotten in. How many *were* there in that group that Xenia had riled up!?

He emptied another magazine, pumping a few dozen rounds into the screeching monsters as they burst into the encampment, looking for fresh meat, and then finally spied an actual, full-on assault rifle on the ground nearby.

Well, he'd have to grab that once this battle was over. As he reloaded yet again, someone suddenly appeared by his side.

"Hey, David," Val said, towering over him with her well-muscled bulk.

She was holding a huge machine gun now, her clothes stained with blood and dirt, her face smeared with ash. She looked like some kind of demon warrior or vengeful archangel.

"Val," he replied.

"Let's kill these fuckers," she growled, and he saw Ashley and another survivor hurry up to his other side.

Overhead and behind him, as he was now on the other side of the hunting lodge, he heard a pistol and an assault rifle open up. All four of them unleashed a solid wave of lead on the encroaching horde of the stalkers.

They came to a dead halt under the combined assault, mainly from Val's gigantic fucking machine gun that seemed to be of the same make and model Vanessa's had been a while ago, the one that had taken drum hundred-round magazines. Val was screaming like a Valkyrie as she unloaded on the stalkers.

Between the six of them, they sliced right through the bulk of the stalkers, and as a solid fifty or so of them were slaughtered in the span of perhaps ten seconds, the surviving stalkers apparently lost their confidence, broke, and ran.

David hesitated. Had he ever seen that before? He couldn't be sure if he'd ever actually seen an undead retreat.

No time for that now.

"I assume you've got a plan?" Val asked, turning to face him.

"Yep. Right now the plan is: gather every bullet, every gun, and every other resource we possibly can in the span of ten minutes, then get the fuck out of here. Ashley, Xenia, I want the two of you on overwatch to see if anyone's coming up on us," David said.

"Yep," Ashley said, heading into the lodge.

"On it, David," Xenia said from overhead. He hadn't even known where she was, but somehow he'd known she would hear him.

He turned as another figure jogged over to him.

"Lori! Thank God," he said.

"It's good to see you too, David," she said, and she hugged him fiercely.

"Oh but not me?" Val asked.

"I knew you were fine you big bitch," Lori replied. She gave David a kiss on the mouth after a moment's indecision. "What are we doing?" she asked.

"Gathering resources. We don't have a lot of time. Grab a backpack and load it down with as much as you can carry, and arm yourself. And get that message around to everyone. I have a plan but we really need to move fast, they're gonna be coming for us."

"Understood," she said. "Come on, Val."

"Yep," Val replied, and the two women headed off.

David looked around for just a moment. The last of the stalkers and Marauders were dead or gone, and this had absolutely been a victory. He could see about a dozen people moving around. Finally, he roused himself, trying to ignore the aches that assaulted his head and his body. He couldn't rest, not yet, not by a long shot.

There was still so much to do.

He got back to work.

...

This was getting to be an intense deja vu for David.

He found himself staring up at the massive mining tunnel yet again, preparing to send another group of people to, hopefully, sanctuary.

"Do you understand the plan?" he asked, returning his attention to Lori, staring her square in the eyes.

He'd told her as they'd headed down into the valley, once he was sure they weren't being followed by anyone. Or rather, once Xenia was sure, as he trusted her senses more than his own at this point. He had checked out each of the people who had been liberated from the hunting grounds encampment. Besides Val and Lori, there had been ten people, eight of them were from Val and Lori's group, two were from Haven, both from Robert's initial group. Some were wounded, but none too severely.

"I understand," Lori replied with a tight nod. "Don't worry David, you can count on me to get people there. And to keep the people there safe."

He nodded, then frowned, looking back at the smaller group that was standing guard a little farther out from the tunnel. Ashley, Val, Xenia, and a man named Fuller who Val had insisted join her. He was tall and wiry and moved with the smooth competence of a warrior who'd been in the shit for a while.

David wanted to send at least one of them with the other group, but he'd seen them in action. They could all fight to varying degrees, and he needed the toughest hardasses on this side of the line if they were going to win this fight.

"All right. Good luck. Stay safe," he said finally.

"You too. Val, we're leaving now," Lori said.

Val came back into the tunnel and David took her place out there. He briefly watched the two women embrace, holding each other and exchanging a few quiet words. And then they let go, and Lori headed off with her group into the darkness, activating some flashlights and disappearing down the large tunnel at a brisk pace.

"Okay," Val said, coming back. "Xenia and Fuller, you're with me. We're gonna go make some noise out in the forest and murder some fuckers."

"Wait, wait," David said. "We need to coordinate. We need something more than just running around like chickens with our heads cut off. You're like the fifth fucking person I've run into who wants to just run around and kill shit. Don't get me wrong, I get it, and I'm not even saying I'll stop you, but we need *some* kind of larger plan."

"Okay, what are you thinking?" Xenia asked.

He sighed and rubbed his head. "We need more people, ultimately. We can get guns, we can get ammo, between the Marauders we ambush and the caches we've got access to guns and supplies. But we need people to actually fight."

"I agree, but what can we do about that right now?" Val asked.

"I'm not sure," he muttered. "We need some place we know to go, let alone some way to communicate. I've got a radio but I'm not sure if it's working and even if it was, how could we coordinate without them listening in?"

"It'd be too risky," Xenia said. "But the reason you haven't heard anything is because they use different channels for each group, so that if one groups gets compromised, they just stop using that channel."

"How do you know that?" Val asked.

"Managed to pull it out of one of them. Not a lot else, though. Whenever I get a few free moments I try a few other channels. Haven't been able to pick up much. I *did* manage to get one squad, they said they were tracking someone near the mountain, by a watchtower, but then they stopped reporting in..."

"Ah. Yes. My fault," David said.

"And mine," Ashley threw in.

Val laughed. "Nice."

"Okay, okay...so, where do we meet?" he muttered. "We need *some* place that we all know about or at least can find easily that isn't *here* because this is already risky enough as it is." He frowned, considering it. Then sighed. "What about River View?"

"We were *just* there," Ashley muttered.

"I know. It's a shitty, miserable place, lots of places to hide, though. They might not expect it and honestly it's about as good as anywhere else..."

"Where is this place?" Val asked.

"On Haven's side of the river," he replied, making sure the three people who didn't know where listening closely, "head upriver, eastward, until you find a road that leads to a partially burned down settlement. It's visible from the river. That's it. Wherever you hide, or tell people to hide and wait, make sure you have a clear view of the end of the main road into town. It terminates in some shacks and a crumbling brick wall. That's where people will go and wait. If no one signals you while you're there, then hide with a vantage point on that spot...Xenia, what is it?" he asked. A look had come across her face, like she had just remembered something.

"Upriver. I just remembered. I saw Ellie earlier today, after sunset."

Ashley stepped forward. "And you didn't think to mention this!?" she snapped.

"Calm down," David murmured, putting a hand on her shoulder. "Where was she?"

"Near the river. She said that she was going upriver, to seek the aid of someone named Azure and her clan," Xenia explained.

David began nodding. "Yeah...that was on my mind, too."

"Who's Azure? What's her clan? More nymphs?" Val asked.

"No. Squids. We helped a clan of squids. Azure's an absolute badass and a bit of a mutant. She can operate indefinitely on land," he replied. "She's a killer, or can be anyway. And I'm positive she would help us. And hopefully some of her friends."

"We have to go after her," Ashley said.

David hesitated, considering it. He knew she wanted to go after Ellie because she was worried about her, but was there a better place they could be? He considered it, then decided no, for once, what was emotionally wanted and what made the most sense aligned.

He nodded. "Okay, you and I will go after Ellie. The three of you, go cause some chaos. But I want all three of you to meet me at River View, and to bring anyone you find that can fight with you, at sunset today at the latest. Katya and Vanessa are out there. So is Akila, I know that for a fact. If you can find them, bring them, we'll need their help."

"With what?" Xenia asked.

"I'm not sure yet, but once I have Ellie, Azure, and whatever other help I can rustle up, we're going to make another strike, just like what we did at the hunting lodge."

"We'll be ready," Val said.

"Remember. Sunset. Good luck."

"Happy hunting," Val said, and then they hurried off.

David looked at Ashley. "Let's go find Ellie."

CHAPTER SEVEN

"David are you okay?" Ashley asked.

He shook his head, making himself focus. It was getting more difficult. "Fine," he muttered. "I'm fine."

"I don't think you are, you look *awful,*" she replied.

He sighed. "It doesn't really matter. We need to go find Ellie."

She pursed her lips as they walked on, and he could tell she was waging a little war in her head. She wanted him to be okay, but she also really wanted to find Ellie, and that must make her feel guilty. "We find Ellie, then take a break," she said.

He began to argue, then sighed. "Yeah, okay," he said.

Because he *was* feeling like shit, and apparently he was starting to look as bad as he felt. He was starting to slow down after the last adrenaline high had really begun to fade out once they'd parted ways with Val and the others.

He felt kind of sick, a little feverish, mostly just slow and in pain. His whole body ached and his head was throbbing, particularly the spot where he'd been hit. He wasn't sure if he *was* sick or just weak from leaping into action and forcing his body to go and go and go after damn near two days of comatose inactivity. And he was no good to anyone if he got himself shot or killed.

As it was, he had been considering holing up at *some* point in the near future, because the sun was now coming up. The first rays of dawn were reddening the skies over the horizon, revealing the thick cloud cover that loomed in every direction. It was probably fifty or maybe even lower than that degrees, a chill wind blowing restlessly across the area. At present, he and Ashley had made it to what he thought of as 'out of the region'.

Basically, past the railroad that cut across the blacktop road that ran alongside the river. When they had first made the journey to Azure's new home, it had been almost six hours. But that hadn't exactly been a quick journey.

They'd been moving with several infirm people, taking breaks and rests periodically. He thought that, if he had to, he could make it there on his own in half the time. Of course, he was really hoping that he wouldn't have to go all the way to the lake. If all went well, they would run into Ellie on her way back with help, and then they could either get to River View or hole up somewhere safe and relax.

Not that he wanted to do even that. They had been talking about executing someone from Amanda's group, publicly. He doubted that was a decision made by that group, but that it was something they'd been told from someone higher up.

And he doubted they weren't going to have an execution just because they'd failed to catch that group. An extremely grim reality that he had been forced to learn at a young age was that you couldn't save everyone. The world was simply too brutal to allow for that.

Everyone died eventually.

And although he'd fight tooth and nail to save as many people as he could, in fact, he'd die to save some of them, he knew he couldn't save them all. Technically, he was sure that he'd already failed to save some. There *had* to be dead among his and

Lori's groups at this point already, incurred during that initial assault.

That had been *their* shock and awe moment.

Fuck them, he was going to make them pay in blood for that.

He grit his teeth as both the physical pain he was feeling and the emotional pain swelled. He thought of Cait, locked up somewhere. Was she hurt? Was their child okay? Something like this was a major reason why he had always assumed he'd just never have children. The kid wasn't even born yet and already he and Cait were having to face the very real possibility of losing them. Fuck. He shook his head.

"I'm sure she's okay, David," Ashley said softly.

He looked over at her. "You can't know that," he muttered, and she grimaced and looked away. Was he that transparent? He guessed not, it would be obvious to anyone who knew him even a little bit why he would be tortured right now.

"It's what I have to believe...about Ellie," she replied, her voice barely above a whisper. "That she's okay. And my family. That they're okay. I haven't seen them in days now and..." She shuddered suddenly and began blinking rapidly, trying not to cry.

"I'm sorry," he said, taking her hand. She squeezed it hard enough to hurt, but he didn't say anything, just squeezed back gently. "I know you're trying to help. I'm just...angry."

"So am I," she growled. "I hate them. I hate them more than I hated the thieves who burned down River View."

"We kicked their asses," David replied. "We'll kick the Marauders' asses too."

"You promise?" she asked.

He grinned savagely. "I promise."

She returned the grin and let go of his hand. Then they both picked up the pace, hurrying as the sun rose on a desolate gray landscape.

...

"Wait. Stop," Ashley said, halting abruptly.

David halted too. He'd heard something as well. He waited, listened. They had been walking for almost an hour now, keeping a brisk pace, sometimes breaking into long jogs. Judging by his memory of the path there, he surmised that they had indeed made it about a third of the way there. So far, they'd come across a few dead rippers and zombies. Perfect headshots, and semi-fresh too. He figured they had to be Ellie's handiwork.

Of course, it could be someone following Ellie.

Then he heard a gunshot, no ambiguity there.

"Shit, come on," he growled, taking off.

There was a path up ahead that veered off to the right. If he remembered right, it led to an abandoned building of some kind. What might once have been a house but had been largely taken back by nature. The road looked familiar and they moved down it.

Even as they did, they heard a firefight break out, several automatic weapons firing and the distinct sound of rippers roaring. Great. Another thing he had to fight that he really didn't feel like fighting. Although it sounded like someone was already doing that for him.

"Wait," he whispered, grabbing Ashley's wrist as they approached the thickets. "Let's do some recon first."

"Yeah," she murmured.

He could read the desperation in her stance, she thought Ellie might be the one fighting.

Shit, she might be.

They slipped into the denser vegetation and then pushed forward until they had a view of what lay beyond, in a large clearing a building lay half-covered in vines and other plants, most of the windows broken out, the roof partially collapsed. Rippers were crawling all over it and he saw a good ten Marauders in the front yard, spread out, taking them down. Well, at the very least, they would get a chance to thin their numbers a little bit more.

"Should we shoot them?" she muttered.

"Not yet," he replied. "The rippers outnumber them. Maybe they can take a few down, then, when it looks like the Marauders have the upper hand, we can open up."

And this was exactly the plan he intended to stick to if he hadn't seen a blue-furred face peer through a section of broken wall in the second story.

"Oh fuck me," he whispered.

"What?" Ashley replied harshly.

"Ellie's there. Second story." He hefted his rifle, the one he'd grabbed at the hunting lodge, and prepared for battle. "Take them out, fast."

"Hell yeah," Ashley growled, hefting her own.

They'd both upgraded their arsenals there. His rifle now came with a scope and a selector for full auto or single shot. He switched it to single shot and took aim at the back of the nearest Marauder's head. He waited for the perfect shot, then squeezed the trigger.

The rifle jerked in his strong grasp and a bullet smashed into the back of the Marauder's head. He collapsed instantly as his brains were ejected out of his skull, flying in a red haze of bone fragments. Immediately, half the force reacted to the gunshot and whipped around, seeking them out. Ashley fired and shot one of them in the chest with several well-placed bullets, dropping him.

Then they returned fire. David cursed and ducked as gunfire stabbed out at him, seeking to end his life. He shifted two steps to the left, knelt, and aimed through a bush. Squeezing the trigger, he shot a female rep armed with an SMG in the thigh.

She screamed, took a few staggering steps, then collapsed. And took aim at him again, but then a ripper got through the others trying to hold them off and leaped onto her, tearing into her body. He winced and shifted aim, putting another five shots into the central mass of another dark-armored Marauder. As he prepared to look for another target, he realized just how many rippers he could see.

There were a lot of them.

They were crawling all over the house and he saw muzzle flare from the partially collapsed second story. Shit, Ellie was fighting for her life. He began targeting the rippers crawling up the sides of the house. He shot one in the head, shifted aim, put two shots into another's arm that sent it sprawling to the ground where it thrashed wildly, shifted aim again and slammed four shots into another's back, splattering the house with its dark blood. As he lined up for another shot, a bullet suddenly winged his shoulder.

He yelled in pain as he felt a burning line of agony tear across his left shoulder. Cursing, he drew a bead on the Marauder that had shot him, flipped to full auto, and emptied the rest of the magazine into the son of a bitch. Hastily reloading, he switched back to single shot, grit his teeth against the fresh agony, (he could tell it had drawn blood), and drew a bead on another Marauder. An examination of the battlefield revealed that there were only three of them left now. The rippers and Ashley had made brutal work of the others.

But there were still a good twenty rippers around.

He put down another Marauder, then joined Ashley in murdering the last two, who were the most dangerous, as they had projectiles. The rippers had to be up close and personal to kill you. With them out of the way, they began picking the rippers off.

"Ellie!" David yelled. "You okay?!"

"David!? Holy shit, is that you!?" she yelled back.

"Yeah!"

"I'm here too, babe!" Ashley yelled, he couldn't tell if she was excited, exasperated, or angry. Or maybe all three.

"Oh my God, Ashley! I love you!" Ellie yelled.

She said something else but it was lost to a fresh flurry of gunfire from her position. David cursed and stepped out of the vegetation, no longer needing the cover. He pumped some more bullets into another pair of rippers tearing their way up the front of the house, dropping them like stones, and then ran dry. As he reloaded, another trio of rippers peeled away and began a dead sprint for him.

He could tell he wasn't going to have time to reload. Dropping his rifle, he whipped out his pistol and opened fire. The first ripper took two shots in the chest and the next caught a round in the neck and another in its malformed, dark-scaled face. He missed the third one, which leaped at him.

He narrowly threw himself to the side, avoiding

it and its awful talon-like claws that gave it its namesake, and heard it crash into the underbrush behind him. Whipping around, he emptied the pistol into the thrashing figure and managed to put it down.

"*David!*" Ashley shrieked.

He spun around. Another ripper was coming right for him. His pistol was empty. He began to reach for his SMG but didn't think he'd get it up in time.

A gunshot sounded and the front of its face blew out in an awful dark geyser of gore. The monster crashed to the dirt and skidded to a halt. He glanced up. Ellie stood by a broken window, smoking pistol in hand, a smirk on her face. She didn't seem feral. She seemed as cocky as ever, which was a relief in a way.

Snatching his SMG up, he hosed down the rest of the rippers still trying to get at them and with Ellie's and Ashley's help, blew them away. David let out a sigh of relief as the last one was put down, then groaned as a throb of pain rolled through his body at the same time that a bout of dizziness hit him.

"David, are you okay?" Ashley asked, stepping closer to him.

"Fine," he grunted, beginning to reload his weapons. "Just go get Ellie. Hurry."

"She can come to us, David," Ashley replied. "Ellie! Get your ass down here now!"

"Coming! Coming!" Ellie called back.

David closed his eyes and leaned forward, resting his hands on his knees as soon as he finished reloading his weapons. The dizziness and headache was getting worse. Actually, his vision was starting to gray out a little.

"David, you need to sit down," Ashley said.

"Don't have time," he muttered.

He forced himself back up, then grabbed his canteen and took several deep drinks. Some of it caught in his throat and he coughed out a spray of water.

"What's wrong?" he heard Ellie asked.

"I don't know," Ashley replied.

"I'm fine," he managed between coughs, putting the canteen back. "We don't fucking have time! We need to gather up this extra ammo and then move..." He hesitated, looking up. His vision had gone blurry and he could just barely make out Ellie coming up to him. His ears were starting to ring and his headache flared again, almost like a snarling beast. "I'm..." He staggered and Ellie rushed over to him as he felt Ashley grab him. "I'm *fine!*" he snapped.

Then everything went black and he was falling.

...

David had dreams that someone was carrying him again.

He didn't like how familiar it was, or how awful he felt. He didn't like the vague yet overwhelmingly powerful sensation that he was forgetting something, that he should be doing something, but he wasn't.

When he finally came to, he opened his eyes to an unfamiliar ceiling.

He heard voices, nearby, two women. Arguing.

Panic ignited in his chest and he sat up with a grunt. Swinging his feet over the side of the bed he was apparently laying on, David planted them on the floor and began to stand up. But he was physically stopped from doing so when the whole world seemed to go sideways, a wave of dizziness washed over him, and his headache flared so bad it seemed to blind him for a few seconds. He groaned and sat back down, then laid down on his side and curled up.

He heard running footsteps and when he opened his eyes again, saw Ellie and Ashley.

"Ellie...oh thank fucking God you're okay," he murmured.

Ellie laughed softly. "It's good to see you too, David."

"I'm still pissed," Ashley said, crossing her arms.

A guilty look came across Ellie's face. "I said I was sorry–"

"Yeah, I know. I'm still angry."

"Shut up," David snapped, causing them both to turn on him in surprise. "Please," he groaned. "My head hurts...fuck, what's wrong with me?"

"You're pushing yourself too hard," Ellie replied. "Ashley filled me in on what you've been up to, and I had a vague idea of what had happened to you after the attack because I do remember stopping by and seeing you and Evie."

"How long was I out?" he mumbled.

"Just half an hour. We carried you to a safe house I set up."

"Fuck, you've got another cache on the way to Azure's?" he asked.

"Yeah, I set it up a few weeks ago. Thank fuck for that. You're dehydrated, exhausted, and overtaxed, David," Ellie replied.

"Obviously," he muttered. He laid on his back and closed his eyes. "Are we safe?"

"Yeah, no one followed us."

"All right...shit, I might need a minute."

"You're taking at least a three-hour nap," Ellie said firmly.

He opened his eyes. "Ellie–"

"Don't *fucking* argue with me, David!" she snapped, which surprised any response he was going to give right out of his throat. Her expression softened. "Believe me, I know. I know you want to keep going. But you need to fucking take a break or you're going to end up dead." Ashley snorted derisively and Ellie sighed.

"Okay, okay. Fine. I'll take a nap, but first, what are you two arguing about?"

"I'm still pissed because Ellie basically abandoned me," Ashley replied.

"All right, Ashley, I get it, you're angry. I'm angry at Ellie for leaving too, but I imagine she had a good reason for doing so. Let's hear her out," he said.

Ashley opened her mouth, then closed it and took a seat in a nearby chair with a huff of irritation, crossing her arms.

"Okay, first off, I'm sorry. I don't...have a good excuse," Ellie admitted. "I kind of lost my mind for a while there. I know, it's not an excuse, but I don't even *remember* when I left you, babe." She looked at Ashley beseechingly.

Ashley's expression softened and she seemed to relax. "You actually don't remember it?"

"*No.* That's what's so fucking scary. I remember being so fucking angry, I was so angry I was seeing red. Literally. I just...lost it. I wanted to burn the whole world down." She hugged herself suddenly. "I thought I was going to lose everything that I had finally, after my whole life, given myself to. After decades I finally, *finally* let my fucking guard down and I let you all into my life, and then these *fuckheads* show up and try to take it all away. It made me fucking crazy. I'm really sorry," she whispered.

"How much *do* you remember?" David asked.

She sighed. "Some. Maybe most. I'm not sure, admittedly. I remember a lot of walking, a lot of running around in the dark, a lot of killing. I just...I'm sorry, okay?"

"I understand," Ashley said after taking a deep breath and letting it out. "I forgive you."

"Thank you," Ellie whispered, walking over to her. Ashley stood and the two women embraced, squeezing each other. Well, that was settled at least. David shifted onto his back and grimaced again. God, he felt like shit. He hadn't drank often, but a couple of times he'd gotten piss drunk and the monster hangover he woke up to in the morning felt like this. Ellie and Ashley seemed to remember him as another groan escaped him.

"Okay, you have to rest," Ashley said. "We're in agreement on that. First off..." She came up with a canteen of water and walked over with it. "Drink this."

"Yeah," he murmured, sitting up a little and draining the canteen. "I should eat too...maybe after I wake up."

"You should," Ellie agreed.

"I'll also need some painkillers," he groaned, passing the canteen back.

Ellie smirked suddenly. "You know, we *could* give you painkillers, and I think we should, but you know what's always been a better painkiller?"

He opened his eyes back up and looked at her. "You two taking turns riding my dick?" he asked, because all at once that lust that had been hitting him again and again, lurking in the background, came back full force.

"I mean...if Ashley's down for it..." Ellie said, looking at her.

"Yeah, I think that's fair," Ashley replied, smiling. "You *did* reunite us."

"All right, though...not too rough. I've got a headache," he replied.

Ellie snorted. "Never thought I'd hear *you* be the one saying 'not too rough' you fucking savage. All the times you've fucking *wrecked* my pussy, or Cait's, or Lara's...you're such a slut."

"Well you all keep wanting to fuck me, what the hell else was I suppose to say?" he replied.

"You're just lucky that we don't get jealous," Ellie said as she took her shirt off, then kicked out of her shoes.

"We *are* safe, right?" Ashley asked as she began stripping as well.

"Yeah," Ellie replied. "Don't worry, I've got great senses. I'll know if anyone or anything is trying to get in. And we're far back from the road, too." She undid her pants and pulled them down, revealing her nude, blue-furred body. "We can fuck in peace."

"That will be nice," he murmured. Naked now, Ellie crouched by her pack and began rooting around in it. He looked down at her fantastically fit ass and her sexy tail swaying back and forth just above it.

How long had it been since they'd last fucked?

It couldn't have been that long ago, but it felt like weeks right now.

And then there was Ashley's smooth, slim, sexy body. He raised his eyebrows a little as she finished stripping.

"What?" she asked, noticing his gaze.

"Nothing you just...filled out a little," he murmured.

"Oh?" she asked, putting her hands on her bare hips.

"Like in a good way, obviously," he said. "You've definitely got more definition. It's hot. I like it," he replied.

She looked down at herself. "Yeah, I had noticed that," she murmured. "You think so?"

"Hell yeah," he said.

"It *is* wicked hot," Ellie said as she stood back up, some painkillers and another canteen in her hand. She walked over to David and gave them to him. "Here, take these, love."

"Thanks," he said, downing four of the painkillers and then passing the canteen back when he was finished.

"Now," Ellie said, setting the canteen aside and then getting down on her knees beside the bed, "lay back and let the ladies take care of you."

"Gladly," he replied.

She took his cock into her hot, wet mouth and began to pleasure him. David let out a loud groan of bliss as Ellie started sucking him off. She bobbed her head smoothly, doing it the way she knew that he liked, given she'd learned how best to please him after all the times they'd had sex. He lost himself in her wonderful mouth, just laying back and closing his eyes. After the stress he'd had to endure, he fucking needed this.

And the hell of it was, he'd had it easy so far. He felt bad, Ellie and Ashley had been out fighting while he'd been laying around knocked out. But right now he couldn't bring himself to do anything but lay there and let her suck him off.

She coated his cock in her saliva, then stopped and quickly mounted him.

"I've *really* missed you," she said as she got into position and slid his cock into her fantastically hot, wet vagina.

"Oh *fuck,* Ellie..." he moaned. "I've really missed you too, *fuck* that's good..."

She groaned in response as she took his whole cock into her. She was so fucking tight and she was as wet as he'd ever remembered her being. She moaned louder as she got comfortably atop him, in the perfect position, then began to fuck him. She was careful, he noticed, but once she settled into that rhythm, that smooth, gentle rhythm, enveloping his cock in a pocket of pure perfect bliss, he lost himself inside of her.

Being fucked by her was absolute paradise.

"Oh wow I forgot how good your dick feels," she whispered, running her hands gently over his chest. He wished his clothes were off. They'd at least taken off his tactical armor, but he still had the clothes beneath them on.

The pleasure washed over him in waves as Ellie fucked him with her stunningly slick, tight pussy. He stared up at her with something like wonder, half-delirious from the fainting and the pain and the insanity of the past day.

She looked angelic, a blue-furred goddess of love and comfort and pleasure. She was smiling down at him, staring at him with her exotically beautiful cat eyes, her left ear twitching occasionally, her eyes wide and alight with furious passion. She leaned down and kissed him, and he hugged her to him, kissing her back. It was a long, wonderful, deep kiss. After a moment, she sat back up.

"It's so good to see you again," she murmured as she continued riding his cock.

"Come on, it's my turn," Ashley complained, sitting at the edge of the bed.

"All right, all right," Ellie replied. She looked glum about stopping the sex but got off of him. Ashley quickly took her place, slipped David into her, and began to ride him just as Ellie had done. "It just feels like ages since I'd had sex. I take it you must've slipped it into Evie at least once before parting ways with her."

"Yes...I did...ah fuck...you know about that?" he asked, glancing at her, trying to maintain his focus in the face of the amazing sexual gratification he was experiencing at the moment.

Ashley's high, firm tits bounced beautifully in sync with her as she put her excellent hips to use. She was crazy wet, too and he wasn't sure how much longer he was going to last.

"Ashley caught me up while we were dragging your heavy ass around. How much fucking muscle mass have you put on since we first met?"

"I'm not sure," he replied, reaching up and groping Ashley's breasts.

"I'd say at least twenty pounds, maybe even thirty," Ellie said.

"What? No way? Ah...fuck yes...shit that feels so good..." he muttered. He blinked several times. He was having a hard time staying focused and, at this point, awake.

"I remember you from back then, you were a scrawny boy," Ashley said with a smirk. "I'm not the only one who filled out. You're in great shape."

"So are you," he murmured, then yawned.

"Okay, David's going to sleep now apparently...who do you wanna finish in?"

"You," he replied.

"Fine by me," Ashley replied as she got off of him. "Less cleanup. And *you* can fucking eat me while he's sleeping."

"Fair's fair," Ellie said as she got back onto David.

He didn't last much longer as the beautiful jag fucked him. In the end, she placed her hands on either side of his head, stared down at him, leaned forward so that her tits hung in front of his face, then began rapidly sliding her pussy up and down his cock.

"Ah *fuck, Ellie!*" he moaned loudly as the pleasure hit him like a hammer.

That was it. He triggered immediately. Grabbing her ass, he started to come inside of her. She let out a cry of pleasure as he thrust his cock deep up into her. She was saying something to him but he couldn't hear her, he was so overwhelmed by the orgasm. The pleasure slammed into him and roared through his body, not just lavishing perfect sexual rapture onto him but burying him in it. Overwhelming him with it.

By the time he was finished, David was teetering on the edge of sleep. He could barely keep his eyes open.

He saw Ellie get off of him, saw her lean in to kiss him, and then he passed out.

CHAPTER EIGHT

When David next opened his eyes, he felt better, but not by as much as he'd hoped.

He shifted slightly and realized that he was being laid on. Twisting his head, he saw that Ellie was stretched out, nude and blue and beautiful beside him. Something had woken him up, though he wasn't sure what it is, and as he was looking at her, her eyes opened up.

"Were you watching me sleep?" she murmured.

"No. I mean, I guess, but not on purpose. I just woke up," he replied.

"Is everything okay?" she asked, sitting up, looking around.

"I don't know."

A second later, they heard a gunshot in the distance. It sounded like a rifle, echoing over the landscape.

"Might be a friend," he muttered.

"Could be, but it's more than likely the Marauders. We don't have many friends this far out. At least none that hang out on dry land for long periods of time." She got smoothly to her feet and began pulling on her clothes.

As David fought the urge to go back to sleep, he felt like he could lay his head back down and pass out again in an instant, Ashley stepped into the room.

"You're up, good. I was just about to wake you," she said.

"How long's it been?" he asked.

"Four hours," she said.

He sighed, irritated, and got to his feet, then began pulling his armor hastily back on. "You said three hours."

"I said *at least* three hours," Ellie replied coolly. "You needed that extra hour. God, you still look like shit."

"Thanks," he muttered.

"No offense, we all look like shit," she said as she pulled her backpack on.

"I guess so," he said.

Once he had his gear back on and all cinched down and secured, he splashed some water onto his face to wake up, then drained the rest of his canteen. He replaced it with some water Ellie had stored at the safe house, then grabbed a pair of protein bars and ate them quickly. He looked at the two women, who looked ready to go.

"Unless something new has come up, we need to go get Azure."

"Still onboard with that plan," Ashley replied.

"Same," Ellie said. "If those fucking assholes hadn't showed up I'd have been there by now. Once we have her and her friends on our side, those shitheads are fucked."

"They're already fucked," David muttered. He began to head for the door, and the other two quickly followed after him.

...

The clouds that seemed to have taken up residence in David's head began to break apart as he left the safe house and hit the path that followed the river once more. There didn't seem to be any Marauder or undead activity in the area, so they set a brisk pace. As they walked, he found himself thinking of Azure. She was probably the most unique among all the people he had met in his life, right up there with Akila.

For the most part, the inhumans had mingled decently well with the humans. He'd come across as many mixed settlements as he had homogeneous settlements that were all humans or all jags or another group of inhumans. By far he preferred the mixed settlements. But even among the inhumans, there were those who preferred to stay away from the populace centers, or those who even needed to. The wraiths, the half-undead, mostly stuck by themselves, but sometimes they lived in or around the settlements, finding places where they were at least tolerated.

The nymphs, it seemed, preferred the woods. He had learned surprisingly little about nymph culture and lifestyle from Akila. She rarely talked about anything that had happened before they met, and he genuinely couldn't tell if it was because it was too painful, or just because she simply didn't want to.

Or maybe there was some unspoken rule among them all that the other races should know as little about them as possible.

Then there were the squids. They had to live underwater. Well, for the most part. He'd never heard of one like Azure, who could live on dry land indefinitely. It had been several weeks since they'd seen each other and he found that he missed her. She reminded him of Akila, though she was somewhat more awkward than the nymph.

Azure was certain of herself, to be sure, but he could tell she seemed to miss social cues occasionally, which made enough sense given squid culture had to be different than human and other inhuman cultures.

She was a skilled warrior, though, and *excellent*

in bed. The women he still regularly hooked up with had all asked him, point blank, at one time or another, who he enjoyed fucking the most. Sometimes it took a few tries, but they eventually pried out of him that it was Azure. And it was mainly because of her vagina.

It was just...*so* wet. And slick. And slippery. And tight. And the texture of it was almost like it had been crafted to perfection for pleasure. They'd had sex a few times since meeting and he had yet to last past a few minutes.

It always blew his mind how good it was.

David decided to stop focusing on sex now that he'd had it with two women recently and instead focus on himself. His body still ached, but it was all a bit duller now, more distant. That was the same with his head. His shoulder though, *that* was bothering him. He looked at it, moving his arm experimentally, and winced.

There had been a lump under his shirt, he suddenly remembered, and it had hurt to put his tactical gear back on.

Ellie noticed him looking. "You got winged," she said. "Not too bad, just a bad cut really. I patched it up, though you'll want to change it before long."

He nodded, frowning. Another injury to throw on the list. How many times had he been hurt over the past seven months?

Too many, although it was more than worth it. David grit his teeth as he was suddenly, violently reminded that Cait was being held prisoner somewhere. Somehow, his brain had managed to turn away from it for a while, like it just couldn't handle it, and it was doing anything it could to keep his thoughts elsewhere. But now she was front and center, and he picked up the pace. The others must have known what was bugging him, because they didn't say anything, just kept pace with him as they made their way down the path.

Under different circumstances, the walk would be pleasant. They were walking through beautiful countryside, past forests and the occasional pond or stream. Sometimes buildings stood off to the side, some obscured by trees and foliage, some destroyed, some surprisingly well-preserved. Even during the winter, which was a time of dying and then frozen death, a sort of icy purgatory, he could appreciate a beautiful landscape.

But not now.

David kept pace in his head. An hour passed and he surmised that they were about two thirds of the way there now. Occasionally Ashley or Ellie would try to strike up a conversation, but it always seemed to sputter and die after a few back and forth exchanges. The silence that followed them was oppressive, broken only by the river nearby. The skies were grayer than before and rain seemed likelier than ever. It didn't matter, he'd keep going, talk Azure and her people into helping, then march right back, get to River View, and wait until the others had arrived, and then they would assault...somewhere. But where?

There were a few choice targets in mind. He wanted to move straight to Haven or the middle settlement, but both were too well-guarded. It would be dangerous and they didn't have enough forces to deal with that yet. Especially not with so many of the bastards out and about, ready to drop everything and go reinforce their friends.

No, it was going to have to be something small. Maybe the fishing village. He didn't want to risk the farm. Honestly, he didn't want to risk any large group of friendlies getting caught in the crossfire, but at some point it was going to come to a full-on assault. What about the military fort?

He needed to do *some* kind of recon. If Lima Company was wiped out, then what had happened to their stuff? Almost certainly the Marauders would've gotten their hands on it all, but maybe they hadn't. Or maybe they'd missed some stuff.

God, was Catalina okay? He'd actually liked some of the people among the military crew. Corporal Cole seemed like a stand-up kind of guy and he'd gotten good vibes from Match and Lina. Were they all truly dead? Or maybe they'd fled. But *how* had this happened?

He was positive they would have heard a firefight *that* massive. God, they should've lit up the night sky defending themselves. Maybe the Marauders had snuck in and killed them all in their sleep? It was possible. Or some kind of poisoning? Though if they had that, why hadn't they used it on the people at the new settlement? Why a direct assault? Maybe they'd run out. Or shit maybe they just liked to mix things up.

There were far, far too many unknowns right now and he just put a cork in it.

They would figure this out later, at River View tonight.

After a while David picked up the pace even more and soon they were jogging down the path. He felt the pressure of time from so many different directions. Every minute he pissed away catching his breath or waiting for the pain to pass or passed out was another minute someone could've been killed. Never before in his life did he so desperately hate the fact that he needed food, water, and sleep. He wished he could just *go* until all the Marauders were dead and all of his people had been saved. But it was an exercise in futility.

He was trapped inside the prison of his own body.

Finally, after what seemed to be far too long for his taste, they came to the lake where they had helped Azure and her clan relocate after they had helped wipe out the viper threat. He came to stand at the spot she had indicated for him, then he began hunting around fervently.

"What are you looking for?" Ashley asked.

"This," David replied, finding a rock the size of a grapefruit and tossing it into the lake about five feet past the shore. It made a good, heavy splash and sent ripples careening across the surface of the water.

"Okay...what'd that accomplish?" Ashley asked.

"Azure told me that if I ever needed to talk to her, to come to this spot and she'd get to me eventually. But she said if it was an emergency, grab a rock and throw it in. That would let her know to come immediately."

"What if it was someone else just randomly throwing a rock into the pond?" Ellie asked.

"She can see very well underwater. If it's someone she doesn't recognize, she evaluates the situation and usually just goes back to her business," David replied.

"Makes enough sense."

David was just about to start pacing by the time Azure showed up, and he was silently thankful that they hadn't had to wait more than a few moments.

"David, Ellie, Ashley," she said, emerging from the water, nude and dripping wet and perfect. She was smiling as she came up onto the shore, but at their grim expressions, she lost her smile. "Something has happened. What is wrong?"

"We've been invaded by a superior force," David replied quickly. "They outnumber us probably four or five to one in total and they've been in control of all our settlements for about two days now. They're armed, violent, and dangerous. Almost all of us are either dead or being held prisoner. We need your clan's help."

The expression that came onto Azure's face made him tense unhappily. She was about to tell him something he didn't want to hear.

"My clan...most of them are still weak or recovering from the experiences with the vipers. And we are so few in number now that we cannot possibly risk any of us. On top of that, it sounds like this is going to be a lengthy conflict, and without safe, reliable access to water..."

He sighed, frustrated that he hadn't realized this earlier. There was the lake, but they couldn't promise that they'd always be able to get there in time if one of her people needed to be submerged in water, and they did *need* it. They would die if they didn't get back into water in time. His mood darkened considerably.

"However," Azure continued, "I will go with you and help you fight."

"Thank you," David replied. Even by herself Azure was a hell of a warrior. "Thank you so much, Azure."

"Of course. We are strong allies...strong friends. You have done so much to help my clan and I, I would do nothing less. Let me inform my people and then we can go to my topside stash and I can gear up, then we can go back."

"We'll be waiting," David replied.

She nodded, and he felt a surge of lust as he couldn't help but see the way the dull sunlight reflected off of her large, bare, wet breasts, or how damned thick and smooth her ass was as she turned away. And he really noticed her nudity as she dove back into the water, disappearing. God, she was so fucking beautiful.

"Wow, she's so hot," Ashley whispered.

"I know, right? She's gorgeous. She's one of the most beautiful women I've ever seen," Ellie replied. "She doesn't really like girls like that, though."

"Ugh, of course," Ashley growled. She shot a smoldering glare at David. "I bet she likes you plenty, lucky fucker."

He chuckled awkwardly, glad to be able to focus on something nice, even if only for a little bit. "Yeah, guilty as charged," he said quietly after stepping back from the lake.

"She's the best lay he's ever had," Ellie murmured.

"Oh *really?*" Ashley asked, raising her eyebrows. Apparently she hadn't been made privy to that particular piece of information.

David sighed heavily. "Yes! Guilty again! I can't help it, she's *really* attractive, and in a way no one else is, but her fucking pussy...it's...I don't even know how to describe it. It's *so* wet and the texture is just...unreal. Fucking her is like fucking a dream."

"Why are you talking so quietly?" Ellie asked.

He shot a glance at the lake. "None of her clan know, and they would be very angry if they found out about us."

"Oh...right," she replied.

Ashley laughed. "Okay, fair enough. And she *is*

probably the most attractive out of all of us, I gotta admit."

"Yeah," Ellie murmured.

Just a few moments later, she reemerged. As she came out this time, however, he realized that the water was rolling off of her quite quickly. Was that something she could control? It hadn't happened the first time, the water had fallen off more naturally and slowly, clinging to her wonderfully toned, curvy body. He made himself focus.

They had finally achieved the next goal, even if it wasn't exactly the outcome he was looking for, it was still a win, and they had to keep those rolling in. The only way they were ever going to win this thing was to hit hard, hit fast, and hit often, and keep at it until the enemy forces bled out from a hundred little injuries.

"Come, my supplies are not far," she said, and began walking towards a small cabin farther down the shore of the lake.

He found himself unable to keep his eyes from her bare ass.

Azure had a truly amazing ass. Wonderfully thick and well-padded, but also very, very fit. He *really* wanted to take her and fuck her doggystyle right there on the shore in the mud, but again, they didn't have time for that.

Maybe later.

"Who are these people who have attacked you?" Azure asked.

"They call themselves Marauders. They wear black armor. They're all armed and pretty well-organized. From what I've been able to gather so far, which isn't much, it seems like they are a very, very large force. What we're seeing may just be a small contingent of them, or it might be all of them. I'm not sure. But the point is there's hundreds of them, they're all armed and dangerous. And it doesn't seem like they'll be willing to surrender. I think this is how they recruit. They take over an area with a show of force, kill some of the people, capture the rest, probably hold them prisoner for however long it takes to break them and get them to join."

"That is terrible," Azure murmured. "Wait here."

They waited outside while she went into the cabin and a few moments later, she came back out with some armor of her own. It was a simple, sleek bodysuit that was padded in a few key places, meant to deflect bullets or knives up to a certain point. She had a pistol on one big, sexy hip, a huge knife on the other, several magazines and grenades, and an assault rifle with a scope and a silencer screwed on.

"You look disappointed," she murmured.

"I just...was enjoying your body," he replied awkwardly.

She laughed. "Do you not enjoy it now?"

"Oh no, you look fantastic, I just...like seeing you naked."

She smirked. "That makes sense. Do not worry..." She paused, shot a glance at the lake, then stepped closer and lowered her voice, "I am sure we will get a chance to take our clothes off together before this is over."

"I'm looking forward to it," he replied.

"Where'd you get all that stuff?" Ellie asked as they began walking back towards the path that would ultimately take them back to their own region.

"I have been scavenging," Azure replied simply.

"Hmm," Ellie said, and apparently that was a good enough answer for her.

David began updating Azure on all the specifics he could think of as they started walking back towards their enemies and their allies.

...

The mood grew a bit grimmer as David provided those updates.

He was glad to see that Azure was taking this very seriously, not that he had expected otherwise. She looked competent and lethal, decked out in her gear and small mobile armory. After he had given her all the information he could think of, and Ellie and Ashley threw in whatever helpful bits they could think of, and they'd answered, or attempted to answer, whatever questions she had, they fell silent and focused on getting back.

That continued for over two hours before David fell into a seemingly unbreakable loop of being terrified that Cait had been killed or Evie and April had been found out and recaptured or killed, or any of his other friends out there, and couldn't handle the silence any longer.

"Azure," he said, garnering her attention, "how have things been going for your clan?"

"Quite well, actually," she replied. She almost looked guilty. "The lake has a healthy supply of fish and plants, which I am finally convincing them to supplement and extend by relying on land-based foods. I have been hunting. They have grown rather fond of deer. I have been training all of them to defend themselves more effectively, and I have a small team of three of the braver individuals who come with me to train to fight and hunt on land.

"I know that there are techniques and, well,

endurance training that can be used to extend the amount of time they can operate without water. At the moment, they can safely operate without it for two hours before they begin to start losing focus. I feel bad, like I am torturing them, which I suppose I *am* in a way, but they're more than willing. We were almost completely wiped out.

"Mostly I try to do the training during rainy days. As long as it is raining, they can continue to operate, and we are figuring out what kind of an extension simply drinking water can give us as opposed to being immersed in it. It's been an...interesting time. And a blessedly peaceful one. Save for one instance where a group of bandits arrived and tried to establish themselves in that cabin so they had a nice little headquarters to rob people from, and some stalker and ripper attacks while we were on the surface, we have been very lucky."

"That's so good to hear, Azure," David replied. "I'm so glad your clan is doing well."

"I appreciate it...*we* appreciate everything you all have done for us. We would be dead now if not for your efforts. And we are doing all we can to rebuild." She smiled. "Three of our number are already pregnant, and three more are trying."

"How about you?" Ashley asked. She hesitated, then sighed. "That was a rude question, wasn't it?" she asked, wincing.

"I do not take offense to the question from you," Azure replied, and Ashley seemed to relax. David was surprised by how far she'd come, really how far both her and Ellie had come, from how rude, inconsiderate, and sometimes outright hostile they both could be. "I am not pregnant, nor do I intend to become pregnant anytime soon. I am afraid that, simply put, I am too useful to them as a warrior than a mother."

"You sound sad when you say that," Ellie murmured.

"I am. I was not sure about how I felt of motherhood before, but after everything that happened, well...I think I would like to be a mother. Unfortunately, it is at present quite difficult to imagine myself with any of the men in my clan."

"Well, you could just use them for a sample, you know..." Ellie replied.

Azure laughed. It was a good sound to hear. "Yes, that is very true. And I am sure most of them would be more than thrilled to donate. It has been...quite obvious to me just how attractive I am to most of the men of my clan."

"Well, you're a really tough, badass, competent woman," David replied.

"Yeah, and how fucking pissed would they be if they knew the only guy nailing you was him?" Ashley asked.

Her cheeks darkened and she ducked her head. "Yes, it would be...bad. I do not think they would oust me if they learned, but certainly they would treat me differently. They rely too heavily on me now. But I am glad I have managed to keep that a secret." She smiled suddenly and reached over, running a hand lovingly down David's arm. "When we find somewhere private...if there is time..."

"Oh yeah," he replied. "I'm so much more stressed than usual and for some reason this whole situation has been making me *crazy* horny. So yeah, I could use it to stay focused. Don't worry, there should be time."

"Good. I have missed making love with you so

very much."

"I guess we should visit each other more often, huh?"

"It *would* be nice," she replied.

Already thinking of being inside of her, David hurried along the path.

...

They made it back into the region without running into much more than a few packs of zombies and stalkers, and dispatching them easily. David was impressed with how quickly Azure reacted, and how accurate her shots were.

She had always been an excellent warrior, but clearly she had been honing her skills down like a fine blade over the past few months. He knew how she felt, although as much as he realized that people relied on him, her group clearly relied on her a lot more than his relied on him. It began to rain, a light misty drizzle that saturated the landscape and muted everything in shades of gray, about half an hour before they got back to the region.

They were maybe a quarter mile from the turn off that would take them to River View when Azure stopped suddenly, and looked to their left.

"What?" David whispered, hefting his rifle.

"Someone's over there," she said, pointing to the collection of trees in that direction. David looked around. The river was to their right, and he didn't see any movement across it, nor behind them or ahead of them, then he nodded.

"Let's check it out, nice and slow."

They shifted quietly off the path and into the woods, which were thick with vegetation and undergrowth. Rain trickled down all around them from the canopy overhead. Occasionally, a bird call sounded, and he caught brief sight of them flitting around up there. It was hard to see much of anything down at the ground level. He felt his anxious apprehension returning as he let Azure lead them and Ashley cover their backs, but he reminded himself that Azure was second only to Akila in terms of her senses.

They found their way to the edge of a clearing, where a lone figure was crouched with their back to them, checking a dead zombie.

David's mouth fell open.

It was one of Lima Company. Or, at the very least, it was someone wearing Lima Company's military gear. Azure glanced at him, inclining her head, letting him know she was passing the torch back to him. She'd found the guy, now it was up to him to figure out what to do next. This was a perfect opportunity to find out what in the hell had happened to the military group...provided this was who David thought it was.

He gently waved the others back just a little bit, then cleared his throat.

"Friendly," he said as the man shot to his feet and spun around, "on your six."

"Get out here, slowly, hands up!" the man replied. He recognized the voice.

"Gator?" David asked as he stepped out, hands up.

The man, who was tall and rangy with a scraggly blonde beard and a somewhat overgrown crewcut, laughed nervously and lowered his SMG. Gator was one of the Marines from Lima Company who had helped during both the stalker and the viper campaigns.

"David," he said. "Holy shit, I thought you were dead."

"I'm not. Gator, what happened? Where the hell is Lima Company? What's going on?" he asked.

"Are you alone?" Gator asked uncertainly, looking around.

"Why?" David replied. Something wasn't quite right here.

"Just like to know who's around," he replied.

"Gator, what happened to Lima Company? I heard some of them talking, the Marauders. They said you all had been 'dealt with' before all this. What happened?"

"Oh, well, uh, about that," Gator replied, reaching up and rubbing the back of his neck, not quite meeting David's eyes. "The story about that is..."

Whatever he was going to say was cut off as someone nearby let out a strangled sound. Both David and Gator turned and watched as another man in military fatigues, his face painted with oil or warpaint or something, came stumbling out, a knife in his throat. He reached for Gator, eyes bugging out, other hand on the knife, then collapsed.

"Aw shit!" Gator snapped.

That was when David heard a muffled gunshot, someone gasped, and then a body fell out of a tree on the other side of the clearing.

"Aw *shit! Shit!*" Gator snapped. He raised his SMG and pointed it at David. "Don't move! Don't fucking move!" he snapped.

"What the hell is going on?!" David asked.

"Never you fucking mind! You bitches come any closer and I shoot him in the fa–"

Another round sailed out of the vegetation and slammed into the side of his skull, sending his head snapping in the opposite direction. David ducked while sidestepping as Gator staggered around like a drunk, his nerves still firing randomly, then he collapsed.

Behind him, Ellie and Ashley had come out, weapons brandished.

"Who the fuck's out there?!" Ellie snapped.

David brought his rifle back up. He wanted to know what in the hell was going on.

"It's okay," a familiar voice said. "We're friends. Don't shoot."

"Catalina?" David asked.

"Yeah, and another friend," Catalina replied, emerging from his left. She walked over to the body she'd apparently made and began tugging the knife out of his throat. From the right, Ruby materialized from the densely packed plants.

"Ruby...holy shit," he whispered. "What's...what's going on?"

"We don't have a lot of time," Ruby replied flatly, crouching by Gator and picking his pockets for supplies. "There's more around. If you have a safe place to go, we should go there now."

"I do," David said. "Is there anyone else?"

"Just us," Catalina replied. She finally got her knife out, made a face, and wiped it on the man's dead body.

All three corpses wore Lima Company gear.

Ruby stood. "Let's go."

CHAPTER NINE

"The Marauders came to us before the invasion," Catalina said as they hurried through the forest, making for River View. "They convinced Stern to join them."

"*What!?*" David hissed.

"No surprise there," Ellie muttered bitterly.

"Yeah, I'm sorry to say it's true," Catalina growled. "We didn't fully realize what was happening until maybe an hour before the attack, when Stern told us all. There was some dissent, and then basically a rebellion. Maybe a fifth of the soldiers rebelled. Some were killed, but ultimately the survivors were beaten down and taken prisoner. Marauder's orders. I managed to slip out in all the chaos. I ran to the settlement, screaming to warn you, but it was too late. The attack started basically as soon as I showed up."

"Thank you, Catalina," David said. "You're a true friend."

She sighed. "Yeah, I just...wish I could've done more."

"We saw your central settlement," Ruby said.

David felt his heart go cold. "Did you see Cait?" he asked, stopping.

"David, we *have* to keep moving," Ellie said.

He sighed and forced himself on. They weren't far from River View now.

"Yes, I saw Cait, she's okay," Ruby said.

"When?" he asked.

"Maybe two hours ago."

He let out a small sigh of relief.

"Lara was there, too."

"Is *she* okay?" he asked.

"Yes. Though it looked like she'd taken a bit of a beating."

He grit his teeth and clenched his fists. "I'm going to give them the fucking beating of their life," he growled. Then shook his head, making himself focus. "What was happening?"

"The Marauders were mostly standing guard. They had your people in chains, but working. They were sorting things, chopping firewood, making repairs to buildings, skinning animals. I think the Marauders are getting ready to move in and they're going to use us all as slave labor."

"Fat fucking chance of that," Ellie muttered.

"What happened to the fishing village?" Ashley asked.

"They attacked at the same time they attacked your villages, I believe. We held out for a while, I was doing good, but Murray saw the situation for what it was. He told me that I was their only hope, I had to get out of there and get help. I realized he was right. I dove into the lake and swam a good distance away, then got to a cache of supplies I had set up, grabbed my rifle and some ammo, and went looking for help."

"But the Marauders were already everywhere, weren't they?" Catalina muttered miserably.

"Yes. They were everywhere. I killed them where I could. Racked up two dozen kills so far but there's always more of them. I ran into Catalina yesterday."

Catalina sighed and shook her head angrily. "She saved me. I was captured during the assault on the settlement. Two Marauders ended up taking me off into the forest. They were going to rape me. Ruby killed one, I killed the other with my bare fucking hands."

"I'm sorry that happened," David murmured.

"Not as sorry as they were, I'm sure," she replied with a savage grin. "I fucking hate these fuckers. I hate Stern so much. I hated Gator back there. He was so onboard with this plan. I saw him shoot one of the ones who was against the plan in the chest, then in the knees. He was a sadistic son of a bitch and I'm glad he's dead."

"We'd been following that little trio for a bit," Ruby explained. "Figured they were up to no good. And I thought–"

They all froze, right near the edge of the forest that let onto the remains of River View, as a distant but huge explosion sounded off. David looked over to the right and he could just make out a large fireball somewhere deep into the forest on the other side of the river. It'd be somewhere north of the bunker, if he had it right.

"Wonder what the fuck that's about," Ellie whispered.

"Katya or Akila or Val stirring up trouble, I hope," David replied. "Come on."

"I assume you have a plan?" Ruby asked.

"Yes. Let's get inside first."

They took a moment to secure the area, but it remained as dead and deserted as it had been the last time they'd come here and cleaned house. David had the others hide among the ruins nearby as he moved to the spot he'd designated.

It was weirder than ever to come back here. He could see his old shack from where he stood, waiting to see if someone would come down and speak to him. Nothing was left in there, he knew it because he'd checked it out one of the times he'd come here, but it was still so surreal to see.

It almost served as a landmark, a place he could come to and visit, and see how far he had come. Because he still remembered who he was back then. He wouldn't call himself a coward, but certainly he had been far more cautious, far more risk-averse.

He'd been a lot more content with much less and he honestly never dreamed that he could be in even half the position he was now. Not the terrible situation the Marauders had caused, but the fact that he was a civic leader, he was in love with several different women, and he was going to be a father. He felt capable and competent in a way he never had before coming here.

No one was coming, he realized, and he waved to the others.

David could ruminate on the past later. For now, he needed to catch some more sleep while he could, because he imagined it was going to be a very long night. There was an apartment building that had been largely untouched by the fires that had initially ravaged the settlement, and although they'd cleared it of supplies, it was still pretty useful for what they had in mind, as it sat not far from David's original shack. It would give them a place to hide and a great view of the area he had told people to wait at.

The group moved up to the second story and settled into an apartment to wait.

While they got settled in, David took a moment to study the women he had with him. When he'd been looking for her, he had to admit that he'd been worried about what state they might find Ellie in.

That she had basically gone feral, and her admission that she had blanked out at least some of the past two days, didn't entirely surprise him. She had always struck him as a woman who was sort of on the edge of crazy. It was really common nowadays, especially among those who didn't stick to a single location and preferred to travel the wilds.

She looked better than he was worried she might though. Standing there, staring out a window with a look of flat concentration on her face, she looked competent and capable. Ashley was in the process of gathering and organizing whatever spare food, medicine, and ammo that people had brought with them so they had a little operating outpost here.

She had held up quite well too. When they had first met, David didn't doubt her bravery, but he did worry that she might be foolhardy and do something that'd get herself wounded badly or killed. Although she hadn't completely shaken that, her stance and her demeanor and movements all seemed to hold roughly the same calm professionalism that Ellie had.

And then there was Azure.

She was like a ninja of old, a calm, living weapon, like she was born for it. She looked calm and smooth and prepared to not only do whatever it took to keep them all alive and intact, but to do it without too much concern. He knew it wasn't entirely true, and thought that some of what gave her that extra air of mystery and precision was the fact that she was not just an inhuman, but an inhuman that was apart from all inhuman races.

It was easy to be mysterious when your culture was an enigma to all others.

Ruby looked calm as well, though tired. The tall, lean, red-furred jag sniper was cleaning her weapon of choice at the moment, her face expressionless, her movements smooth and professional, like she'd done this a thousand times before. No doubt she had. David was tremendously grateful to have her back in the fold.

Besides being an exceptional shot and a great warrior, he'd grown to like her much, and she him. They hadn't spent a lot of time together, but she had let him know that she liked him and his closest friends far more than most of the people she lived with. He'd trust her with his life, and had already more than once.

Finally, Catalina. Although he hadn't had as much of a chance to get to know her all that well, he had enjoyed the time he'd had with her. And not just because they'd slept together. She still had a sort of youthful enthusiasm, and was a bit naive, but he'd always thought her heart was in the right place. And apparently he'd been dead on the money, given what she'd just told him.

She seemed the most anxious of the group, doing a decent job at keeping a lid on it and appearing calm, but now that the adrenaline was gone, he could tell.

David himself sat down in a nearby chair and felt the energy leave him. After several firefights and six hours on the road, most of it hurrying, he didn't feel entirely up to facing the reality that they were actually facing a worse enemy than he'd initially thought.

The revelation that Stern had turned on them shouldn't have been a revelation at all, and yet...he was still having a hard time believing it. Although the guy had always been a condescending dick as long as David had known him, he genuinely believed that he wouldn't ever do something like this. Even after the way he'd ducked a responsibility he'd committed to a couple months back and Lara had finally split from Lima Company, this was still a surprise.

Stern more seemed the type to fight a group of

fascist dickheads who jacked off to the idea of 'might makes right' tooth and nail, to the bitter end. He seemed the type who would rather die on his feet than live on his knees.

David shook his head, another priority taking up residence in his brain once again.

"Ruby," he said, looking at her.

"Yes?" she replied without looking up from her rifle.

"You said you saw Cait and Lara? How did they seem?"

"As I said, Lara was moving slowly, and she had a black eye. It seemed like she had been given the job of bringing the workers water to keep them from passing out. Cait wasn't restricted in any way, no chains, but she did have a guard with her. She seemed like she was talking to people, comforting them maybe. She didn't seem hurt in any way."

David felt relieved, but simultaneously enraged.

And worried given what Catalina had told him about the Marauders.

It killed him that they were going to have to wait for sundown, but he didn't want them to risk getting split up, or injured, or killed, or captured. Not when they had this much fighting potential in one place, and more was on the way. Hopefully. So he forced his mind away from that thought, taking a moment to calm himself down.

He felt another wave of pain and lethargy hit him and knew he needed to rest. It was the most logical thing to do, and if anything, it would make night come faster. From his perspective, at least. He looked over at Azure.

"We should have sex and then those of us that could use sleep should get it," he said.

"I am okay with that," Azure replied.

"Who stands guard?" Ellie asked, then yawned.

"I will. Today, nor the past several days, have been taxing for me. I was actually resting before you came to get me, so I am ready and fresh. I will watch over you while you sleep," Azure said.

"Thank you so much," Catalina murmured. She rubbed one eye. "I'm so fucking tired."

"Get some sleep," David said, standing up and walking over to Azure.

He took her hand and began leading her out of the living room, towards a bedroom in the back. He hesitated as he realized literally everyone was following them.

"Is there...something I can help you with?" he asked uncertainly, lingering in the hallway that connected the bedroom to the living room.

"If you think there's a chance we're missing out on an opportunity to see you and Azure in action, you're sorely mistaken," Ashley replied.

"That is, of course, if Azure is okay with it," Ellie said, a bit more tactfully.

"I am," Azure replied with a smile. He had an idea that she had grown to like all the attention.

"I guess at this point I shouldn't even be offended that you don't think to ask me," David said as he kept walking into the bedroom.

"Come on, David. You love getting watched while fucking as much as we love watching you while you fuck," Ellie said.

"Pretty much," he agreed.

The bedroom still at least had a bed, a decent queen size that could comfortably fit three of them, uncomfortably fit four. He shrugged out of his pack and kicked his boots off. They could figure out sleeping arrangements later. For now, he just wanted to be inside of Azure, enjoy her smooth, very slightly slick gray skin against his own, taste her unique taste as they kissed, and revel in the unparalleled bliss that was fucking her sweet inhuman pussy. Both of them quickly stripped down naked and got into bed.

"Someone needs to keep watch," he said.

"I will," Ruby said.

He noticed Catalina was staring and blushing fiercely. He grinned at her. "You gonna be okay?" he asked.

"I...yeah," she said, clearing her throat and looking around, then blushing more. "It's just, uh, been a while since I've seen people, you know, fuck."

"I'm still down to sleep with you if you want," he said.

"I...yeah. I'd like that," she murmured, surprisingly shy.

"We'll find some time," he said, and then he was kissing Azure. She kissed him back with an immediate and immense passion, getting right into it without hesitation. Azure was a passionate lover, he had found. His hand found one of her firm breasts and he groaned at the feel of it. Groping her, running his hands over her, was truly a pleasure all its own. She slipped her strange tongue into his mouth and he tasted her immediately. It was a welcome return. He let out a groan of his own as her hand found his cock and began to massage it.

"I *have* missed you tremendously," she whispered between kisses.

"Oh I've missed you too," he replied. "So very much."

She smiled and opened her legs. "Show me."

Okay, no preamble then. Fine by him. He got in

between those thick, well-formed thighs and laid his head at the entrance of her slick vagina. Azure's whole body shuddered and she let out a very satisfying to hear moan as he penetrated her, sliding slowly into that slippery, tight opening. And again he was hit by that sheer impossible pleasure, the shock of how *good* her vagina felt, as he got all the way inside of her.

"Oh, wow. Azure. Oh my God," he whispered as he started stroking into her.

She let out another moan and adopted a satisfied smile, looping her arms up around the back of his neck as he held himself over her.

"That I can cause this reaction in someone, especially someone that I admire so much, is quite gratifying," she said, staring up at him with those strange dark eyes of hers. Her teal hair was longer than before, though just as messy as ever.

"He likes your pussy best," Ellie said.

"They're jealous of you," he panted, then moaned again. The pure sexual gratification of her slick, slippery pussy sleeved tight around his cock, baking it raw ecstasy, was becoming too much. Fucking Azure was practically a religious experience.

"I am sorry, though...not *that* sorry," she admitted with a sly grin that quickly dissolved into an open-mouthed expression of ecstasy.

Ellie laughed. "Hey, I wouldn't be either. At one point *my* pussy was the best he'd ever had. Then it was Akila's. Then it became yours."

"Hmm. I provide greater pleasure than Akila. Even Cait?" she asked.

"I'm not answering that," he panted, barely following the conversation as he stared down at her firm breasts bouncing in sync with his thrusting, at his cock disappearing into her perfectly smooth inhuman vagina again and again.

"Tell me, I wish to know," Azure pressed.

"You're better, but only just. When Cait got *really* pregnant that put her head and shoulders above the rest. Pregnant vagina is *amazing,* and it's just barely an extremely close second to you now. You've got an unfair advantage, I think. You're a squid." He sighed, shook his head. "Come on, don't make me feel bad. I don't judge you all by how good you fuck."

"Of course not," Ellie replied. "Being good in bed isn't the end-all, be-all, David. We know that." She hesitated. "Well, most of us do. I know it. Cait knows it. Evie knows it. Lara and Akila know it. I can tell you that much. There's so much more to relationships, but...it *is* nice for some of us to keep score, you know?"

"I must admit, I had not thought of it much before meeting you all, but I do like it. Although perhaps that is because I have an unfair advantage," Azure said, then she moaned loudly.

"Not so loud," Ruby murmured.

"Sorry...David feels...*so* good..." she moaned, biting her lower lip and putting her legs in the air. "Oh yes. Yes...David...right there. Oh right there that is *perfect...*"

"Holy fuck, Azure, I'm not going to last long. This is seriously the best fucking pussy I've ever gotten in my life," he whispered, almost incoherent with pleasure again.

"I understand...I am close..." she whispered, and reached down between them.

She began to rub her clit, and he felt her whole body shudder and twitch, and she bit back a louder cry of bliss. He kept screwing her, hitting that sweet, sweet inhuman vagina raw, enjoying every second of burning hot pleasure that ate into him, filled him, consumed him. She managed to make herself come within about ten seconds, and he managed to last perhaps two seconds beyond the point where her extremely wet orgasm began.

David lost himself in the way her already tight vaginal muscles constricted around his dick, massaging it furiously, and the hot, wet spurt of sex juices escaped her, and her whole body convulsed in bliss as she held a hand over her mouth, muffled moans of total rapture escaping her. He groaned loudly, falling down against her and hugging her tightly to him, thrusting madly into her, burying his entire length into her as he started shooting a load inside of her.

He pumped her pussy full of his seed, just absolutely filled her up with it in hard spurts. The pleasure that blasted through him was unusually powerful, like a volcano erupting or a seismic event. Some kind of tremendous explosion of pure, mindless paradise.

He wasn't sure how long he filled her pussy with his seed or the orgasm raged through him, but when it was over, he was left shaky and sweaty, trembling in its wake.

David opened his eyes, staring down at Azure, his face an inch from hers. She smiled at him and kissed him on the mouth. "I really like you," she murmured.

He laughed softly, kissed her again. "I really like you, too."

"I must clean up, and prepare for guard duty now," she said.

He nodded and pulled out of her, then laid on his side. He felt the bed shift and glanced over. Ellie laid down beside him.

"How we gonna handle sleeping arrangements?" he asked.

"Well, obviously Ashley and I are gonna sleep here with you," Ellie replied.

"I am comfortable with the couch. I believe Catalina would like to join you," Ruby said.

"Well...yeah," Catalina said, still looking embarrassed.

David waved her over. "Well, come on then. We need to sleep while we can."

"Will you spoon me?" she asked. "I could really use that right now."

"Of course," he replied.

She set her gear aside and got out of her boots, then climbed into bed, laying down beside him, her back to his chest. He put an arm over her and held her against him. She settled more comfortably into his grasp as Ellie did the same thing with Ashley.

"Thanks for being nice to me, even though I had to stop seeing you and Stern turned into an asshole even before all this shit happened," she murmured.

"You're a good person, Catalina. I've always known that." He kissed the back of her head. "Whatever happens, you can count on us. Okay?"

"I...okay," she said, sounding relieved. Deeply relieved. He had to imagine she must have spent a lot of time terrified out of her mind over the past few days. Not just because she was almost raped or taken prisoner, but because her entire support system had not just collapsed before her very eyes, but had actively turned against her.

That had to be terrifying.

So he held her, and did his best to calm her, to let her know that as shitty as it all was right now, he was here for her.

They were all here for each other.

He fell asleep almost immediately.

...

When he came awake, at first, it seemed like nothing at all had changed, and his initial impression was that he'd woken back up after fifteen minutes.

But then he realized two things: he actually felt more rested, and the quality of the light coming in through the broken window of the apartment had changed.

It was darker.

It was also no longer raining, though the skies he could see were still gray. Azure hadn't moved from the spot by the window, almost like a statute.

He heard movement behind him and carefully disengaged from Catalina, who was still asleep as far as he could tell, and rolled onto his back. On the other side of the room, he saw Ellie and Ashley crouched by their packs, sorting through them, gearing up.

"What's happening?" he murmured.

"It's almost night," Ellie replied. "We should be getting ready. I was just going to wake you up in a few minutes."

"Okay," he said. He rolled back over and felt Catalina stirring. He laid a hand gently on her shoulder and ran it slowly down her arm. "Hey," he murmured.

"Hi," she said, then yawned. "Are we okay?"

"We are okay. There has been no activity...though I have heard much distant fighting, but it stopped about an hour ago," Azure said from the window.

"Hopefully it was Val and the others deciding it was high time to meet us here," David said.

Catalina rolled onto her back and looked up at him. "If we've got time, can we, uh..."

He grinned. "Yeah, we've got time. If we're quick."

"I can be quick," Catalina replied. She sat up and shed her shirt quickly, then her bra, freeing some wonderful tan breasts. "Can I do reverse cowgirl? I don't know why but I *really* want to do that with you."

"Fine by me," David replied.

She stripped with an eager impatience and all but leaped onto him once she was naked. She began kissing him immediately. It had been a while since he'd hooked up with her and he had honestly missed her. She was a very attractive woman and, of course, women in military fatigues apparently got to him hardcore, and she looked just as good as ever. She slipped her tongue into his mouth as she pressed her nude body against his own.

His hands wandered over her, touching her breasts, her wonderful hips, the swell of her ass, her fantastic thighs. Soon he was fingering her, and she moaned loudly into the kiss as he slipped a finger into her and began pleasuring her intensely. She was wonderfully wet inside.

After just a few moments of this, she decided enough was enough, it was time to fuck. He let her mount him, watching her get into position, facing away from him. He got a good look at her hot, fit ass as she reached down between them, gripped his cock, and rested it at the entrance of her pussy. He could feel the heat coming off of her. She moaned loudly as she penetrated herself with his cock and he listened to her moan and gasp as she worked him into herself.

"Damn, that's hot," Ellie said softly.

"Yep," Ashley agreed.

David lost himself inside of another fantastically beautiful, fit woman as he watched his cock disappear all the way inside of her slick pussy. It didn't take her long to settle into a good rhythm and then she was just fucking him, fucking herself with his rock-hard cock. He laid back, hands behind his head, and enjoyed the ride.

They didn't fuck for very long. It was easier to last with a human pussy, even one as wonderful as Catalina's, but he also didn't have much of a problem in pushing himself into the orgasm. He let her fuck him until she got herself off and a little ways into her own orgasm, he pulled her against him and started coming inside of her.

They both moaned and writhed in bliss, lost in the dark depths of their climaxes, and when they were done, she took a few seconds to collect herself, then got up off of him, found some water and a rag and some soap, and began cleaning herself up.

"Thanks," she said. "That was awesome."

"Right back at you," David replied as he sat up.

After that, it was all business. He managed to wash, dry, dress, and grab a meal before Azure told them that someone was coming. David hurried over to join her and saw that someone had emerged from over the wall. He recognized that tall, bulky figure.

"That's Val," he said. "She's a friend. Get everyone ready, I'll go get our friends."

He grabbed his rifle and hustled down the stairs. Once he got to the main entrance to the apartment, he let out a little whistle.

Val snapped her rifle over in his direction, then lowered it. "David," she said quietly. "We good?" she asked.

"We're good. Who else is here?"

She turned and let out a little whistle of her own. He saw several more figures emerge from either over the wall or through the opening he himself had used earlier. He saw Xenia, Fuller, and Katya join them.

"This everyone?" he asked, slightly disappointed. He'd wished for more, but it would do.

"Yeah, couldn't find anyone else," she replied.

"All right, let's go."

They hustled into the buildings after making sure they weren't being followed and went up the stairs and back into the apartment.

"Ellie, good to see you, I heard you went a little nuts," Val said with a grin as they walked in.

Ellie chuckled ruefully. "Yeah, you could say that. I'm all here though."

"Quick introductions. Val, Fuller, Xenia, this is Azure. Azure, these are members of the new group of people I told you about on the way down here. They're quite capable."

"Damn straight," Val murmured. She looked Azure up and down. "Wow, I could just tell from the way David talked about you that you must be wicked hot but *damn* you are beautiful."

"Thank you," Azure murmured.

"Not into girls," Ellie said.

"Fair enough. My compliment stands," Val replied with an easy shrug.

"Let's focus," David said. "Did you find anyone else? Akila? Vanessa?"

"No sign of Akila," Katya replied. "We found

Vanessa and she helped us with an attack, actually. Lured a good dozen Marauders into a place we used some C4 we had stashed away for a rainy day planted in and blew them to hell."

"So *that's* what that was," Ellie said.

"Yep. They're *dead*. We tried to convince Vanessa to go with us, but she said someone needed to stay out there and make us seem like we're bigger than we really are, especially if we're all gathering up in one area to mount an assault," Katya explained.

"That actually makes sense," Ruby murmured.

"Okay, so...lemme think a minute," David muttered, considering the situation. "Everyone from the farm is pretty much at the farm, and everyone from the fishing village is there, except for Ruby, who's here. Barring the people we know who are here, or on the island, or are captured, that means...huh, yeah, it would just be those two left out there."

"Unless someone managed to slip away," Ellie said.

Ruby shook her head. "No, our recon showed it was locked down really tight. It's unlikely anyone else slipped away."

"We *did* manage to find a couple of my people who'd been hiding out in the wilderness," Val said. "I sent them to the island." She looked at Catalina. "So who's this?"

"Catalina," David replied. "Remember the military company I told you about? Turns out they weren't wiped out, they betrayed us. They're working with the Marauders."

"Well fuck," Val said.

"Not *all* of us did," Catalina, stepping forward.

"No, some rebelled. You said they were taken

prisoner, do you know where?" he asked.

"Yeah...some of the recon we did earlier today was at the dockyards. They had the prisoners there. There weren't too many but...I'd really like it if we could get them back."

"Who was among them?" David asked.

"Cole for sure. And Lina, I think. And I think two or three others."

David considered it, then nodded. "I think she's right. We know the dockyards decently well. And we've got an advantage: Azure can attack from the water. They think that lake's empty now, because it is, they probably will be lax lakeside. Between all of us, I think we can pull off an attack and rescue operation. What do you think?"

"I'm game," Val said, and Fuller and Xenia nodded.

"I'm in," Ellie said.

"Same," Ashley said at almost the same time.

"We'll need a good plan," Katya said uncertainly. "I imagine it'll be well-guarded."

"It is," Ruby said. "I think I have an idea. Remember our assault on the thieves at the hunting ground last year? I was thinking we could do something similar."

David nodded. "All right, let's hash it out, then get ready for battle."

CHAPTER TEN

The plan was about as good as it was going to get, David felt.

At present, he was switched on, amped up, and ready to shoot some monstrous fuckers in the head. True night had fallen and the thin misty rain had returned, saturating and muting everything. He ran through the plan in his head again as he hurried through the dark woods, keeping an eye out for Marauders and undead.

Ruby was going to find a nice, safe spot and snipe for them.

Katya and Catalina had agreed to setup a kill zone in the woods, a place where everyone could run to once they had the prisoners, if they were still alive. Then the survivors could dig in and kill whoever was following them. David was going to lead Ashley and Ellie in one team, while Val was going to lead Fuller and Xenia in another team. Between them, they had managed to get enough watches to sync them and put together a basic plan.

Ruby would get into position and wait until David's team and Val's team were both in position as well, one to either side of the dockyards. Once the window of time had passed to where the two teams were supposed to be in position, Ruby would start sniping.

She'd keep it up until the alarm was raised. The second that happened, both teams would launch a pincer strike at the same time, and whenever she thought it best, Azure would rise from the lake and start taking people out. Their main goal was to get to the prisoners and extract them, while killing as many enemies as possible. It was definitely one of those things that could go great or horrifically.

Recalling what he knew of the dockyards, David had figured that the most likely place for prisoners to be kept was the storage warehouse. The bunkhouse was too useful, and the dry-dock and utilities building were too important to keep people who wanted to kill you, or at least damage your stuff, in.

Which just left the sheds and warehouse. He'd told all this to Val, who was to investigate the sheds first, quietly, if possible, and make sure they weren't there. It felt unlikely, but it *was* possible. She was coming in on the utilities side, he was coming in opposite, near the storage warehouse. That was his intended target.

As they slunk through the trees, approaching the edge of the forest, David couldn't help but notice how good Ashley had gotten at moving quietly. She'd always had a bit of a knack for it, but she'd definitely improved. And then there was Ellie. She was like a ghost. They crept up to the edge of the trees and he checked his watch.

They only had a few minutes to get into position, but it should be fine. The dockyards were lit up off to his left, as obvious as a bonfire in a pitch-dark night. He could see a lot of activity going on.

According to Ruby, who had also done some recon on the dockyards earlier, they didn't have any people from their settlements here doing grunt work, just Lima Company. Which was a little humorous in its own way. Maybe they had to prove themselves. Besides the prisoners, there should be nothing but hostiles around.

Or what Val had referred to as a 'target rich environment'.

He didn't see anyone on the road or in the field beside the dockyards. They set off, slipped across the road, and started to move low and fast through the field. It was a bad place to be and they were heading for a little rise in the land about twenty feet shy of the structures. They could at least lay down flat and out of sight there for a bit. He could already see a few people standing on top of the bunkhouse, keeping watch.

They got to their destination and laid down flat without a problem. Ashley kept watch for stalkers or anything else that might want to sneak up on them in the night, while he and Ellie scoped out the situation as best they could. David glanced up briefly. The moon was out, but it and the stars were largely obscured by that same cloud cover. It had lingered all day long, dropping rain on them off and on, as if the region itself was weeping over what had happened. David checked his watch again. It was basically go time.

They waited.

As they watched, abruptly, one of the three men on the roof of the bunkhouse collapsed. The two others turned to face him and began walking towards him, and faintly, just barely, he could hear them asking what was wrong, what had happened.

The rearmost sentry fell next, jerking violently to one side.

God*damn* Ruby was a good shot.

He wasn't even sure where she was, but he thought she was in the forest, maybe up a tree. Not the *best* position to snipe from, but apparently it was working. The final man had time to turn around before he took a bullet to the brain and the life was splattered right out of him.

"Showtime," David whispered, "let's get closer."

The three of them rose as silent as death in the night and began creeping closer to the dockyards. He just barely caught sight of a faint flash of light far off to his left, in the forest. They kept going, listening, tensing for that moment when the alarm was raised and all hell broke lose. They didn't have to wait very long.

As his group came within maybe five feet of the edge of the concrete the dockyards were built into, someone shouted, and then someone else yelled, and then there was gunfire. And then there was a *lot* of shouting and gunfire.

"You two, go cause chaos! I'll get into the warehouse and try to find our friends!" David said.

"On it, good luck!" Ellie replied. "Come on, babe!"

Ashley went after her as she headed for the bunkhouse. David hustled over to the back of the warehouse. There had been a back entrance there, he remembered coming across it the last time they were there. It had been almost rusted shut, but had they gone to the trouble of opening it, or had they decided to leave it that way?

His silenced pistol out, David hurried over. As he got to the door and reached out to grab it, the knob suddenly twisted and it was thrown open. He raised the pistol and fired the second he found himself staring at a Marauder.

The surprised look stayed on the man's face even as the bullet punched through his forehead and he dropped to the ground, half-in, half-out of the warehouse. Was he fleeing or just coming to cover the rear exit? Didn't matter either way, David supposed, and stepped over the body and into the warehouse.

Lima Company had made some changes. There was a lot more stuff in there now, a lot more crates, and a shooting gallery and makeshift gym had been established. He saw a few people rushing towards the front exit and let them get to it. It sounded like absolute and unfettered anarchy out there right now. He hoped the others would be okay, but he had an idea that they might not all be walking away from this one unscathed.

Or maybe even at all.

Which was why he had to hurry. David scurried along the wall, running for all he was worth, until he reached the stairwell that led to the second story. There was a really good chance, in his mind at least, that they'd be up there. Of course, it was possible that they'd just up and murdered the survivors, but he didn't think so.

They seemed big on enslaving people. David got to the top of the stairs and leaned out into the hallway that ran the length of the second story. No one there, but there were a lot of open and closed doors along its length. Was it really a few months ago that he was here, helping Lima Company take the place from the vipers?

Seemed like years.

He moved up to the first door and leaned around, gun at ready. An empty office. He moved on, checking the next door. An almost totally empty room, save for some boxes shoved in one corner. As he prepared to move on, a door opened and a man in a dark camouflage uniform stepped out, holding a pistol. He froze as he locked eyes with David, who was already pointing his pistol at him. This wasn't anyone he recognized.

"Wait–" he said as David pulled the trigger.

The round hit him in the eye and he dropped like a rock. A second later, another door opened and a man stepped out, a shotgun in his grasp, and David shot *him* in the eye as well. Another rock dropped. He couldn't be sure if these were Marauders and this was what they wore under their armor, or if this was Lima Company and they'd changed their uniform. He shook his head angrily as he kept moving and clearing rooms.

There *was* no more Lima Company.

They were *all* Marauders now.

And they would pay for what they had done.

David had hesitated at the idea of revenge, of vengeance and retribution before, but he no longer did. Not now. He didn't know if it was just his anger speaking, his almost maddened protectiveness towards Cait and Evie and April and the others, but he didn't think so. There was no way to coexist peacefully with the Marauders, they had made that very clear. It was their way or death. And David had no intention of dying.

As the fighting outside intensified and something exploded, he finally came to a door that was locked with a metal bar across it, held in place by a padlock.

He hammered on it. "Anyone in there?!"

"Yes!" a muffled voice called back almost immediately. "Who is that?! We're being held prisoner! What's going on out there?!"

He recognized the voice but couldn't place it.

"It's David! Stand back from the door, I'm getting you out of there!" he said.

"Understood!"

He waited five seconds, then fired the shotgun he'd snagged in passing from the second dead

Marauder. It blasted the lock right off, he yanked the bar aside, and kicked the door in. And there, inside a room with iron bars welded over the only window, he saw four people, three of which he recognized.

Corporal Cole had helped them out a lot during the stalker incident, a squat but well-built man. He'd apparently ditched his short, maintained hair for a shaved head. His previously calm eyes now held a manic edge

There was also Lina, the technician who had helped them repair the boat that ultimately allowed them to mount the assault on the island during the squid campaign. Tall, thin, and with an air of grim stoicism, her glasses were cracked and she had a bandage on her head. The final member that he recognized was a young man who called himself Match.

He had helped David during the last stand on the island against the squid army and although he'd stayed with Lima Company, obviously he hadn't stop being a decent individual. He looked older now, his hair a bit longer, his face gaunter. He looked angry and miserable.

The final person in the room was a man of average height and weight, decently fit, with a red crewcut and a sour expression. The namepatch on his chest was damaged but still legible. It read *PFC Tennyson*.

"Is this it? This is all that's left of the rebellion?" David asked as he stepped back and hustled them out of the room.

"Thanks," Cole said as he accepted the shotgun David gave him. "So you heard about that? Yeah, it's just us. I think Catalina made it out but..."

"She did, she's why we're here. Come on, you're

the whole reason we mounted this assault. Let's get you armed and get the fuck out of here."

"You heard the man, let's *go* people!" Cole snapped.

They hustled back down the hall, and Lina paused briefly to scoop up the pistol the first dead man was still holding.

"There's guns in the shooting range, and ammo," Cole said as they hurried down the stairs.

"Jesus man, sounds like a world war out there!" Match marveled. "How many people you managed to find for this attack!?"

"Not enough, they'll need help," David replied hastily.

"Shit," Tennyson muttered.

"We can handle this. I assume you've got an exit strategy?" Cole asked as they jogged across the warehouse, wary of anyone who might've slipped back inside, but the place still seemed as empty as when David had first crossed it.

"Yep," he replied. "We're all heading for the forest directly across the street from this place as soon as we get our people out."

"Understood."

Using his shotgun, Cole bashed open a gun locker, then stepped over to the next one and repeated the action. "Load up!"

The other three immediately hit the gun lockers and started snatching the pistols and rifles that were stowed inside.

"We gotta hurry," David said, glancing out the door.

"We need our body armor," Cole replied, hurrying off towards a collection of crates nearby. "I think I saw them put some...here! Come on, everyone!"

David kept watch while Cole and the other survivors of Lima Company hustled over to the crates, pried them open, and began pulling on the body armor with a quick proficiency. He found himself immensely grateful for their presence and professionalism. If there was ever a time he needed people trained to kill, it was now.

Once all four of them had pulled on their gear and snagged their rifles and pistols, he had to admit, they looked the part. He didn't think it was going to be easy now, but maybe they might not be *as* fucked.

He looked out the main doors again carefully. From what he could tell, the others had managed to get themselves pinned down in the central building, the dry-dock. The Marauders had it surrounded, it seemed, and he could clearly see Val, Ellie, Ashley, and Fuller, but he didn't have a perfect view of it all. Shit, they had to get in there, and fast.

"All right, we're going to overwhelm them from the back, get our people out of there, then cover their retreat, got it!?" David asked hastily.

"Understood," Cole replied.

"You cool with following my orders?" he asked.

They all nodded.

"We've seen you in action," Match replied.

"Then let's get some payback."

David led them out, sweeping left and right to make sure there was no one to either side of them, but it seemed that all of their attention was presently focused on the dry-dock. Perfect. David and the four Marines lined up and opened fire at roughly the same time. The Marauders didn't know what hit them.

The bullets slammed into them from the rear and the screams of agony immediately overwhelmed all the other noises that were being generated. He saw Val take notice of what was happening and she quickly redirected the others to focus fire on the other two sides they were being hit from.

David poured fire into a trio of Marauders that had been crouched behind a row of metal crates and emptied the magazine putting them down. As he snapped out the magazine and slapped the next one in, he saw some of the Marauders trying to turn around to return fire. They were fast, but Cole and company were faster and more brutal. They had to be enraged, infuriated, absolutely livid, and it showed in their actions. David shot a Marauder in the head, watching the blood come out in a spray to join the misty rainfall.

He shifted aim and put a slew of five rounds into another's chest, sending the woman stuttering violently backwards where she toppled over a crate and fell onto her back. One leg stuck up in the air. It didn't move.

Blood flew in the rain.

Bodies were pumped full of holes and toppled to the ground.

Shell casings began piling up.

David burned through two more magazines before they had finally managed to clear out not just the Marauders on this side of the dry-dock, but the others who kept trying to show up and reinforce them. Every now and then one would slam forward unexpectedly, half their head disappearing in a grotesque explosion of gore. Ruby still doing her work without pause, without hesitation, without fail each time.

"Cover me!" David screamed, and took off at a dead sprint towards the open side of the dry-dock.

He saw Val crouched down behind some crates, doing something. As he drew up to it, yelling over the gunfire, he took it all in at a glance and realized that he could see everyone. No, check that, almost everyone.

He couldn't see Xenia.

"Let's go! We're pulling out! Now! I've got them!" David screamed.

"You heard him people! Get the fuck out of here!" Val roared as she stood up suddenly, holding a bundle in her arms.

His eyes bulged as he realized what she was holding was not a *what* but a *who*.

Xenia.

There was a lot of blood on her and her eyes were closed. Jesus fucking Christ, was she dead? He couldn't tell, but he thought Val was a practical enough person that she'd probably abandon the body if Xenia was dead in a situation this extreme. Or maybe she just didn't know one way or the other, and wasn't willing to risk it.

Cole and the others had moved forward, towards the end of the dry-dock building that was nearer the forest, and was firing at a collection of Marauders there. It was going to be a bitch to get back to the forest, David knew.

Really, it was a gamble. There was too much open space. But he had one more ace up his sleeve. He looked back and saw that everyone was out of the dry-dock now, strung out along its metal, rain-slicked wall, waiting on him.

"Get ready for it!" David yelled as he hurried up to the corner of the building, where Cole was blind-firing.

"For *what!?*" he demanded.

David pulled out his ace. "This!"

"All right, ready!"

He'd managed to find and tape together a flash-bang grenade and a fragmentation grenade. He pulled the pin on both and hurled it around the corner, at the largest collection of Marauders who were pinning them down, and pulled back around.

There was a chorus of screams that all disappeared amid a brilliant flash and a thunderclap of explosive sound.

"Go! Go! Run!" David screamed.

And then it was chaos. Just chaotic, frenzied madness as the whole lot of them ran for all they were worth towards the treeline where Ruby was, and where the kill area Catalina and Katya would have established by now was.

Several of them fired in passing into the confused mess of stumbling Marauders, trying to eliminate as many of them as possible without sacrificing any speed or time. David hastily counted heads as he ran for the road. Ellie and Ashley were there. There was Val carrying Xenia. Cole and his three charges were still together, near the rear, covering them. There was Fuller, who had fallen in with them.

That was everyone.

Provided Xenia was going to survive, they might get through this without too much of a problem. Of course, they had to actually get out of it first.

They had barely begun crossing the road when concentrated fire started coming their way. David fell back to join the others near the rear to fire back over their shoulders at the Marauders and try to get them to scatter long enough for them to hit the woods. If they could get into the trees, there was a good chance they could get away.

For several hectic, terrifying seconds they ran their asses off, just booking it across the cracked pavement of the road, then hitting the dirt in the stretch of open land that separated the road from the forest, and then finally they made it to the trees.

"Go! Keep going!" David yelled, digging in his heels, skidding to a halt, and turning around. He looked at Cole and the others. "Follow them!"

"Go!" Cole yelled, and skidded to a halt beside David. So did Fuller.

Everyone else kept on sprinting into the forest. Standing among the treeline, the three of them raised their weapons, three different models of machine guns, and opened fire. There were still a good fifty Marauders moving around over there at the dockyards. Granted, probably a quarter of them were injured, but that was still a shitload to deal with.

He opened fire, letting out several bursts and sending the advancing Marauders scattering for cover. He managed to drop one of them, then dropped to one knee, stabilized himself a bit more, and kept firing. He didn't have to keep this up for that much longer, just enough to give the others some time to get back and establish the kill area a bit more solidly. Then they could run.

The first magazine ran out and he managed to put down another two Marauders. As he reloaded and fired a few more times, he began to think it was time to get going.

"All right–" he started, then was interrupted by an awful wet splatting sound and a spray of something hot against the side of his head and then he heard a solid thump. Turning, he saw Fuller had collapsed. He was laying on his side, his eyes wide open, a hole in his forehead.

"Fuck!" Cole snapped.

"Fall back!" David yelled. He emptied the magazine, then turned and began sprinting away through the trees.

He reloaded as he and Cole ran their asses off.

"Where are we going?!" Cole asked.

"Trust me!" David snapped back.

Cole either trusted him or didn't want to waste breath asking further, because he just fell silent. They ran on through the trees. It was difficult to navigate, but David had gotten to know these woods pretty well. They ran until they hit a big rock with a pointed tip in a clearing, with David occasionally firing over his shoulder, and then they skidded to a halt in the clearing. He looked around, just caught sight of Ellie peering out from behind one tree, and Ruby behind another.

"This is it, hide," David replied. "We're gonna catch them in the crossfire."

"Perfect," Cole replied.

They split up and found hiding spots. They waited, listening. It didn't take long for the Marauders to come after them. There was shouting, a lot of it, and some gunshots as they were no doubt running into any undead in the area that had been drawn in by all the chaos, lots of flashlights swaying through the trees as the larger force came after their attackers.

David couldn't help but grin savagely.

They might be a larger force, but they were about to be a raging river meeting a goddamned immovable boulder.

They would break upon it.

And break they did.

The very second they crossed the threshold and enough of them had gathered in the clearing, intending to pass through it no doubt on their way to hunt down their enemies, David and all the others opened fire from their concealed locations.

It was a slaughter.

Guns roared in an overlapping wave for almost sixty complete seconds. David went through two full magazines and as he reloaded the third, the gunfire stopped so they could take assessment of the situation.

Judging from the awful sounds coming from the clearing, a few had survived. David felt his gut twist. Although he hated the Marauders for all they had done, (he had no doubt that a group this big, this savage, and this ruthless, had a long, bloody history behind them), he didn't think he had much sadism in him.

He didn't want to see them suffer.

"Ruby, Ellie, Catalina, watch our backs! Everyone else, put them out of their misery and grab whatever you can!" David called.

"Katya, I need your help!" Val snapped.

"Help her," David said, seeing that she was crouched over Xenia.

They all set to work.

Over the next few minutes, a gunshot would ring out occasionally as they found one of the survivors and put them out of their misery, or as an undead showed up, looking to get in on the murder themselves. David could hear more of them out there, both undead and Marauders, and knew they didn't have much time. He was hoping the darkness and the undead would keep the Marauders busy enough to give them time to escape.

David grabbed as much spare ammo and weapons as he could manage, shoving several into his pack, and killed two Marauders before deciding he'd done enough. He hustled over to where Katya and Val crouched over Xenia, and that was when he got an idea of how bad it was. He saw they'd already patched up her right shoulder, though it was already bleeding through the bandages, and they were in the process of dealing with two gunshots wound in her guts.

"Jesus," he whispered.

"I'll be fine," Xenia managed, looking like she was clinging to consciousness.

"Jesus Christ, Xenia, fucking let yourself pass out!" Val snapped.

Xenia opened her mouth to argue, then sighed and relaxed, closing her eyes, apparently agreeing to Val's demand.

"Give her some morphine," Katya replied distractedly.

"How soon until we can move her?" David asked.

"I need at least another five minutes," Katya replied.

"Fuck!" David snapped, considering it.

He could hear more Marauders coming, and not just from the initial direction, either. It sounded like some were on their way from the new settlement as well. This was going to get bad.

"Where's Fuller?" Val asked.

"Dead," David replied flatly.

"God*damnit!*" she snapped.

"What are we doing here?! We're about to have company!" Cole called.

"Fuck!" David growled. He leaped back to his feet. "Ellie, Ashley! Guard them! Lima Company survivors, Azure, here, now!" Everyone quickly gathered around them. "Cole, you remember where that bunker is? Over across the river?" David asked.

Cole thought for just a second, then nodded. "Yes, I know where it is and how to get there," he replied concisely.

"Good. I want you to take your squad, that includes you now Catalina, and start heading in that rough direction. You're a distraction. Lead the Marauders away from here, and then when you lose them, get to the bunker and wait for me there. Understood?"

"I understand, we'll get it done."

"Good luck," David said.

Cole nodded tightly. "You too. Let's go!" he snapped to the others.

The soldiers hustled off.

David looked at Azure. "You're with me, we're distraction number two. We're heading towards the mountain. Ellie, get them to the mine entrance and *wait for me there.* Do you understand?" he asked, staring hard at her.

She looked like she wanted to argue, but he held his eyes with hers, almost trying to will her not to argue with him. She shot out an exasperated sigh and nodded once. "Yes."

"Keep her alive, keep yourselves alive," David said. "Let's go, Azure."

CHAPTER ELEVEN

It took three long, harrowing hours to work their way back to the mining tunnel.

David and Azure led the Marauders who ended up coming their way on a merry chase. Initially they began to have real trouble losing them, as the Marauder squad that was on their asses was tenacious and probably furious, but ultimately they managed to lead them right into a pack of stalkers, and that had been enough.

They'd swung by the cave where Ellie had stored some stuff and David grabbed some more medical supplies, as well as some explosives he'd tucked away there at one point during summer, and then they'd left.

From there, they'd made their way across the region, through the forest, then over the river, then plunging back into the dark woods once more. All the while dodging angry patrols of Marauders. It was like they'd shaken up a hornet's nest. On the one hand, David felt great for dealing them a serious blow, on the other hand, he was frightened. This might push them to do something violent and cruel in retribution. They fucking deserved to be murdered, but his people did not deserve to suffer for his actions.

It just meant they needed to go faster.

The longer this stretched out, the bigger a chance this had of going wrong. Well, even more wrong than it already had.

They finally hit the bunker and found Cole and his squad waiting there for them, undamaged. Once the two groups had linked up, they'd hustled over as quickly as they could through the chill, misty night air to the valley, down into it, and at last to the mining entrance. He was terrified that they wouldn't find anyone there, that something had gone wrong, that Xenia would have died while waiting for them to show up.

But they were there.

"Identify yourself," a familiar voice called out.

"It's David and friends, Ellie," David replied.

A sigh of relief. "Get over here."

They hurried over and David turned to the others. "Cole, take Catalina and Match and Tennyson and form a perimeter, watch our backs."

"Understood," Cole replied.

David had to admit, he was deeply relieved. He thought there might be some resentment there between the former members of Lima Company and himself, but they all seemed fine with him and his friends.

He brought Azure and Lina over to join the others, and found them all there. Val was sitting on the ground a little ways inside the tunnel, Xenia's slim form in her lap and arms. Katya was standing with Ashley, Ellie, and Ruby closer to the entrance.

David looked at Xenia unhappily. "She's out of the game, isn't she?"

"Yes," Katya replied flatly. "She's down for the count. If she gets rest and someone tends to her, she'll make a full recovery. She's tougher than she looks. But she *needs* to get somewhere safe and out of the way."

David sighed softly. This was bad. Xenia was likely one of the most skilled and deadliest among them. At least one person was going to have to take her to Helen's house, almost certainly two. He had already updated Cole and his friends on that particular situation, and he'd been bouncing ideas around in his head on the way here. It was time again to weigh between keeping warriors here and sending good fighters to the island to keep it safe, just in case, especially with more wounded on the way. He made his decision.

"Katya, I want you to take Lina and get Xenia to the island," he said.

"What? No, I'm not stepping out of this," Katya replied. "And you need me over here, anyway. I'm the only qualified combat medic among you."

"No, I know probably as much as you do," Val replied. "He's right. If we're going to be sending wounded your way, we need all the medics we can get on the way there."

"You at *least* need to be at Helen's place to protect it and stabilize people if they show up bloody," David said.

Katya grit her teeth, looking around at them, then her shoulders slumped. She nodded slowly. "Fine. Goddamnit. Just...end this quick, yeah?"

"Yes," David replied firmly. "I intend to. I'm really counting on you, Katya."

"I know, I know." She laughed softly. "Didn't you turn out to be quite the leader?"

"I guess so," he replied. He shrugged out of his backpack and had Azure do the same. "Lina, Katya, open your packs. I'm sending more medicine and ammo with you."

They quickly transferred some of the contents of their packs and then Katya took a moment to check over Xenia again. Once she seemed satisfied with the bandaging, she carefully picked her up, as she was the stronger between her and Lina.

"You ready?" she asked the engineer.

"I'm ready," Lina confirmed.

"Good luck," Val said as she stood.

"You too."

The three of them disappeared into the tunnel. Val moved to join David. "What now?" she asked sourly.

He noticed a lot of her vicious cheer had gone out of her and didn't blame her. Fuller was dead and Xenia was out of the picture, as was Lori.

David let out a little whistle and Cole and the others hurried over.

"Anything?" he asked.

"We're clear," Cole replied.

"Okay. We need to come up with another game plan. That went well...I mean, as far as it was expected to go. But we need to strike while the iron's hot. They're in chaos right now and probably aren't expecting another attack. Or if they are, they're out looking for us. Where could we realistically hit next?" he asked.

"We should take control of the military base," Cole replied immediately. "That was one of the first things I was intending to do if I got free. There's a secret route inside almost no one knows about. Just me and Lara really."

David frowned. "What secret route? How doesn't Stern know about it?"

Cole sighed. "I found it maybe a week before Lara left. I was checking the coastline nearest the fort for viper activity, off by myself, and I found a pipe, a big one. It was open, built into the natural wall of the lake, but obviously meant as a runoff pipe. It's got maybe just a few inches of water in it. I decided to check it out.

"Got inside. It runs all the way to the base.

There's a hatch that lets into an old storage room that we basically never go into, underground. I was going to tell Stern, but at that point I was getting worried. I told Lara instead. She told me not to tell anyone else and she'd figure out what to do with the knowledge. I'm guessing she never told anyone else."

"She never mentioned it to me," David murmured.

Cole sighed. "Lieutenant Hale is strongly...loyal isn't the right word. Moral, I guess. She was right to leave, but I don't think she ever expected anything like *this* to happen." He frowned bitterly. "None of us did. Maybe she felt like she shouldn't bring it up unless there was an emergency, and obviously never got the chance to tell you. Either way, we know about it now. We should use the advantage."

"I agree, but slipping in unnoticed might not be enough," Ellie said.

"So let's do what we did before," Ruby suggested.

"You really think we should repeat exactly what we did before?" Ashley asked uncertainly.

"That's probably what they're thinking. 'No way they'll try *that* again'. Plus, misdirection is a perfect tactic, honestly," David replied.

"Okay, so what then?" Val asked.

"Azure, Cole, and myself go in through the pipe. Ruby, get to a good location and snipe. Val, I'm going to give you some explosives I got my hands on. I want you to blow the back door wide the fuck open. That alone will cause a lot of chaos. Catalina, Ashley, Ellie, Tennyson, and Match will back you up, Val. You'll be the big distraction. Pretty much just kill as many of them as you can. My group will come up from the back and hit them from that direction. We kill until they're all dead or fled, and the base is ours," David said.

They took a moment to hash it out a bit further, then made sure they had synced watches and worked out a timetable, then checked over their guns one more time and rushed off into the darkness, making for the military base.

...

David was getting tired.

Even with the rest he'd been getting, he wasn't supposed to be going for this long. *Especially* after being comatose for two days. He could feel the toll it was extracting from his body, and his mind. But it wasn't like he had a choice. He *had* to keep going, keep pressing. The best way to kill off a superior enemy force, from what he'd gathered, was to keep hitting them, keep them off balance, whittle them down bit by bit.

He hoped Akila and Vanessa were out there, doing good work.

The rain had let up, but the clouds still lingered. He was presently following Cole with Azure along the shore beside the lake, heading for the pipe in question. David knew he could keep going, he knew he could probably push himself for quite a while longer, but he wasn't entirely sure what his limits were, and he didn't want to pass out in the middle of a battle or while having to run his ass off from an undead or a Marauder.

I've been through worse, he told himself.

Like that time he'd been bitten by a fucking squid. God, what a nightmare that had been. He still sometimes woke up with nightmares of his skin sloughing off and his eyes melting and his brain rotting as he turned into a rabid animal and tried eating the ones he loved the most. That he'd been through worse helped, somewhat, but not as much as he'd hoped. David held grimly onto his focus as Cole muttered to them that they weren't far.

Up ahead, in the dim moonlight, he could see a curiosity in the landscape that rose above the waterline. He didn't see anyone around, but it was clear there was a lot of activity going on all over the region. No doubt dozens of groups of Marauders were out and about, looking for the ones that had so thoroughly embarrassed them.

David hoped they were running into undead and traps set by his allies. One good thing that might come out of this, he realized as they came to stand over the pipe's entrance, was that once this was all said and done, there would probably be way fewer undead roaming around for quite a while.

Having five hundred armed assholes roaming the land for several days might have that effect. And once the Marauders were gone, they might be able to enjoy a week or maybe even two of relative peace and quiet.

They were going to need it.

"Here it is," Cole said. "Best way in is to lower yourself down. Let me just look inside and make sure it's safe."

He laid down flat on his stomach and scooted forward until his upper torso was over the top of the pipe. David held down his ankles to keep him from falling in.

"Okay," he said, and David let go. Cole sat up and then began the process of maneuvering himself over the edge and down. "It's safe, far as I can tell.

I'll go first."

He lowered himself, gripping the top of the pipe, and then swung himself inside. Azure went next, the most graceful of them all, clearly. And then it was David's turn. He put his back to the lake, held onto the pipe, and lowered himself. Beneath him, the water lapped gently against the pipe and the natural wall it was built into.

It smelled bad, but at least it wasn't overwhelmingly awful. David gave himself a little swing and let go, landing in ankle-deep water with a small splash. Cole had a flashlight on its lowest setting several yards into the pipe.

They set off.

David found himself wanting to ask questions of Cole. Why had Stern agreed to this? Why had so many of the others agreed to it? Did Stern really hate the other people in the region that much? Did he think it was the best choice? The moral choice? Had he been coerced? That seemed unlikely, but possible.

Did Cole know any of this? Maybe not. It seemed like the kind of thing Stern would have just come out with, just told them all one day like it was another order. The less of a chance you gave people to think about something, the less you presented it as a choice, the less likely they were to question you about it.

But now wasn't the time for any of that.

The clock was ticking, and lives were on the line.

Now more than ever. If the Marauders had been planning on executing people as an example before, they were certainly going to be that much more pressed to do it now. David tried not to think of it. He had to keep pushing, keep going, keep killing. Eventually, it would be over. Eventually, they would win, and the faster he did it, the sooner it would come. Of course, if he tried to go too fast, he might end up getting himself killed.

Or worse, someone else.

He could still see Fuller lying on the ground, eyes wide in shock, a bullet hole in his forehead, leaking fresh blood.

They splashed through the pipe until Cole suddenly held up his fist.

"Wait here," he said, and splashed off.

David turned on his flashlight. He could see the end of the tunnel maybe five yards ahead. He turned the light down on his watch. They had about two minutes before Ruby started up with her sniping. It was basically the same plan as before. By now, Val's team should be in place. Ruby would take out any sentry along the back once the two minutes went by, then someone from Val's team would sneak up and plant the explosives. They would have one minute to get the job done.

If possible, Ruby would hold off on sniping for that sixty seconds. Once it was up, she'd keep going, and then once the alarm was raised, Val would blow the explosives and they'd mount the assault. David and his people were to stay in reserve until the chaos had started. As the first minute passed, Cole came back.

"Okay, come on, I don't hear anyone and it doesn't look like it's been tampered with," he said, then began leading them back.

They followed and came to the hatch. David checked the watch. The final minute went by. "Okay, open it," he said.

Nothing changed, but he almost expected to hear something, despite the fact that they were underground. With a bit of effort, Cole got the hatch open, twisting a wheel, his large biceps bulging with effort. It squealed a little, making David wince. Once it was open, Cole slipped through, then gave the all-clear. David and Azure crawled in behind him. They came into a dank, dingy storage room that looked like it hadn't been used in ages. Everything was covered in a layer of dust and there was a lot of water damage on the walls.

"Door's over here," Cole whispered.

They followed him around a big stack of ancient crates, past a pair of shelves packed with all sorts of random, useless items and junk, and came to the only door in the room. They gathered by the door, waiting. David checked the watch one more time, watched it until the final minute had looped around, and then waited some more.

"I hate doing this," Cole muttered.

"I'm sorry," David replied. It had to be hard, attacking what used to be his friends, what used to be his home. "But it—"

"Has to be done, I know. I regret that it has to be done, but I don't regret doing it. Not now. Not after all I've seen." He sighed miserably.

Suddenly, gunfire, muted but obvious, broke out. Almost the second it did, a tremendous explosion ripped through the area. David felt it almost like a punch in the chest as the concussive force blew down into the earth. The whole area rattled and several things fell off the shelves. Dust flew into the air. Immediately, more gunfire roared to life.

"Let's do it," David said, throwing the door open and stepping out, rifle at ready.

Cole had already given him a basic description of the layout and where he needed to go to get up, not that it was particularly difficult anyway.

They came into a hallway with lots of water damage and now flickering lights. They split up and opened each of the doors there. Cole warned him that occasionally this was where people snuck off to catch a nap or just be out of sight for a while, and it was more than possible that the Marauders would want a full inventory.

The battle overhead intensified as they cleared it, finding no one among the old storage rooms. Once that was out of the way, David led the charge up the stairs at the end of the corridor. He kicked open the door and came into a large, open room that served as the entryway into the main structure of the fort.

He saw half a dozen people in various states of preparation on mounting an assault, and, recognizing a few of them, he opened fire while sidestepping. Barely a second later, a second barrage of gunfire sounded as either Cole or Azure, whoever had been behind him on the stairs, got up there and joined him in the battle.

The Marauders managed to get a few shots off, but none that connected. They were gunned down quickly, six more dead bodies to add to the dozens, maybe hundreds that were laying all over the region now.

"Azure, stay here, guard the door," David said. "Cole, with me, help me clear this place out."

"Yep," Cole replied, and headed off towards one of the doors along the back of the room.

David's heart was hammering in his chest, blood was roaring through his veins, laced with adrenaline that gave him a high of terror and anxiety and excitement, all mixed hopelessly together. All around him, the awful sounds of battle raged. Mostly it was just guns firing and people screaming. Sometimes screaming orders, sometimes screaming in agony. Something exploded, though with no more force than perhaps a grenade.

He and Cole moved through the first floor, clearing out mostly living areas. They moved with a brutal quickness, checking everywhere someone might have hid, (though that seemed unlikely), and they managed to get through a pair of bunk rooms, a shower area, and a mess hall without running into anyone.

No doubt everyone was either out there doing the Marauders' dirty work or now defending themselves from this surprise attack. Once the first floor was swept, they hurried up the stairs to the second story and got back to it.

David pushed a door open and stepped into an infirmary. It was empty, thank God. He wasn't sure if he could bring himself to shoot someone laid up in an infirmary, even if he didn't seem to have as much difficulty executing wounded on the battlefield. Would they show him the same courtesy? Maybe, but only so that they could enslave him or perhaps get him well enough for a public execution at this point.

Cole was checking out some offices. David moved on, opening another door and clearing a small storage closet with a sweep of his rifle. He kicked the next door open and found himself in another office, what might even have been Stern's office, possibly. Two Marauders, both of them former Lima Company, as they were still in their fatigues, whirled around as he kicked the door open. Both were armed, and both had been firing out of a window. He drew a bead on one but thought that he was only going to have enough time for that first shot.

David fired.

The burst hit the man square in the chest, ripping through his uniform and releasing a huge spray of blood as the force of the blast sent the man stumbling back and smashing through the remains of the window they'd been firing out of.

David turned to fire a second burst, but he could already see the second man had lined up his own shot and was getting ready to fire.

Suddenly his head snapped forward as a bullet exploded out of it the same second the remains of a second window burst inwards. He collapsed immediately, gun clattering to the floor. Ruby, David realized in an instant. Saving his ass. He was frozen, still as a statute, for a few seconds as he realized how close he had come to death. He was going too fast, and this was the risk of going too fast. Shaking it off, he finished double-checking the room, making a note to come back here soon, as no doubt Stern hid some useful shit in his office, and rejoined Cole in the main hallway.

"You okay?" he asked.

"Fine, how much more is there?" David asked.

"Third floor and that's it. Once we're up there, we can help your people. There's probably no one up there right now," Cole explained.

David nodded and they hurried on. They ran up a flight of time-worn metal stairs and came to an open room with several doors along its edges. The pair split up, moving to the nearest doors and opening them up. Moving more cautiously this time, David cleared the room, found it empty, and moved on to the next one. He and Cole repeated this three times each and at last found themselves in a building they controlled.

"Let's do it," David said.

They got to the best vantage point, opening up some windows that gave them a view of the courtyard, which was where most of the soldiers seemed to be gathered behind sandbags and other makeshift barriers and barricades. The first and most obvious problem for his friends that he saw was that the watchtower by the front gate was occupied. Ruby must be busy elsewhere. He prepared to take it out, but then Cole got his attention.

"David, might be time for an upgrade," he said, and nodded to a desk beside him.

David turned and looked, then his eyes widened. There was a single body in the room with them, and it became obvious to him what that person had been doing when Ruby's bullet had sought and found his skull. Another assault rifle lay on the desk. It was almost the same make and model as the one he currently had, but with one amazing upgrade.

It had a fucking grenade launcher slung under the barrel.

And there were custom little grenades meant to fit into it lined up on the desk beside it, as well as several magazines. David abandoned his rifle and snatched up that one, loaded it up with both bullets and a grenade, and then took aim at the watchtower, which he was just a bit above.

"Fire in the hole," he muttered, and fired the grenade.

It sailed through the air in a beautiful arc and connected directly with the watchtower, which went up in a massive fireball that briefly lit up the night sky. David laughed, a little wildly, his eyes wide, trembling in adrenaline-hyped excitement, and he hastily grabbed a second grenade and loaded it up. Looking down into the courtyard, he saw that the

Marauders there might have had a pretty decent chance of winning, even caught with their pants down. Only that was about to change, and change hard. Already some of them had put together what was coming next and were beginning to scatter, trying to escape.

He could see his friends firing on them, taking advantage of the chaos.

David targeted the biggest cluster of hostiles and let fly the second grenade. That did it. Those who weren't incinerated were sent flying through the air aflame. And that was the exact moment that their defense fell apart, and whatever chances they might have had to save themselves ended right then and there.

From there, it was a simple matter of just cleaning up the survivors. Between Val and her team on the ground, David and Cole up top, and Azure, they picked off those who were still alive one by one.

Mostly, though, these were just acts of mercy.

As soon as he no longer saw any of them moving around, he and Cole hurried back downstairs to join the others. Once they got to the ground floor, Azure joined them in leaving. They met back up with Val and her team and he was relieved to see that they were all still alive, breathing, and mostly intact. Val had obviously been winged by a bullet, her right bicep bleeding freely, and Match had been grazed on his left thigh. They were both in the process of patching themselves up.

"Okay, now what?" Val asked while she worked.

David sighed. He'd been considering that over the past few minutes. "It's obvious that we can't hold this place for ourselves. We're a mobile force, we do best with lightning strikes. And this place is just too important to let fall back into their hands. Maybe if we could get most of the gear out, but there's so much important shit here..."

"So what are you thinking?" Ellie asked.

"Let's blow it up," he said, then looked around. There were a few looks of surprise, but he was glad to see that most of the others accepted it almost as soon as he said it.

"I love that idea but let's do one better," Val said. She looked up as she finished smoothing the bandage into place over her wound. "Let's grab as much shit as we can, plant the explosives, and then blow it when the Marauders come looking to take it back."

"That's a great idea, double the damage," Cole said immediately.

"Okay. Soldiers, you know where the best shit is. Val and Azure, go with Tennyson. Ashley and Ellie, go with Match and Catalina. Cole, you're with me. Grab the best guns, the best ammo, the best gear and medicine and food you can find, as much of it as you can safely manage. Do it fast as hell. Cole, show me where there's enough explosives to blow this place to hell."

"I know how we can do this," Cole said, and headed off back into the building.

Everyone split up and got to work.

CHAPTER TWELVE

They only risked working for fifteen minutes.

Cole showed him a surplus of C4 charges that Stern had kept locked up in his own office. Lucky, he'd left the key behind. David wondered if the man was now numbered among the dead out there. He thought he'd seen him during the fighting, but he couldn't be sure. Either way, he supposed it didn't matter at the moment. Once they had the C4 and the detonator, Cole brought him down to where they had a supply of natural gas.

"This is going to wipe out the entire base and some of the surrounding land," Cole muttered as he set the charges.

"I hate to lose this place but..."

"Yeah, we don't really have much choice."

Once the charges were set, they rushed back outside, gathered up whatever they could for themselves among the dead, (David had swung by the armory and managed to get a few more of those grenades for his launcher), and then they fled the military base. They rushed across the open space between it and the nearest forest, where Ruby would be up. He could just make out her slim, red form high up in a tree, perched expertly.

"Stay up there!" David called as soon as they reached the base of the tree. "Tell us when you see any Marauders coming to the base!"

"Got it!" she replied.

"Now what?" Val asked. She looked about as exhausted as he felt.

"We have to keep the pressure on, but we need to do some reconnaissance work. I want to break up into little teams and check out the region. Both to ambush Marauders but also to see where they're at and also to see if we can find Akila and Vanessa. It's time to bring them back into the fold. If we play our cards right, we *might* be getting to the point where we can launch a major offensive and finally turn the tide," David said.

"What? How?" Cole asked. "They still outnumber us like twenty to one, probably thirty or forty to one."

"What about all the people in the fishing village? The farmers? Haven? My and Val's people at the new settlement? You think just because they've been taken prisoner or agreed to a ceasefire they're beaten and out of the game?" David replied.

A thoughtful expression came across Cole's face, and he nodded slowly. "Based on what I've seen when we were working together to deal with the stalkers and then the squids, you all are pretty hardcore. The fight can't be kicked out of all your people yet."

"Yeah and you never even *seen* my people in action," Val said.

"So you think we launch an attack, they'll rise up?" he asked.

"That's what I'm thinking. It'll take some coordination, but if we move fast, hit hard, and get lucky, we might be able to end this whole thing today. We'll execute every last one of them, and then we'll have our land back. Our homes back," David answered.

They were all silent for a few seconds, considering that.

Finally, Val nodded. "Yeah, I'm in. We can't let this drag out. So let's divvy up the land and split into teams and do recon."

They took a moment to get it all figured out, who would go with who and where.

He ended up deciding to stick here with Ruby, because no one had shown up yet, and someone needed to stay behind, even if just to blow up the empty base.

Cole went with Catalina.

Tennyson went with Match.

Ellie obviously went with Ashley.

Azure went with Val.

They agreed to meet at the (now abandoned) hospital after a few hours of scouting. David watched them go and then waited, the minutes passing by. He sat down heavily, putting his back to the tree that Ruby was up. He wasn't sure how much she had heard, but no doubt she knew he'd update her on what she needed to know what she came down.

After about five minutes, she spoke up.

"David...I see them coming. A big group."

He grinned savagely and got back to his feet.

...

David sighed. It had been a long, long four hours. A good fifty Marauders had mounted an assault on the base, looking like they were trying to go in by force. Several of them hurled flash-bang grenades over the wall and then rushed it, only to find a lot of corpses and a few fires still smoldering. David had waited until most of them were inside, then he'd hit the detonator and blown all fifty of them straight to hell.

After that, he and Ruby had hurried off, doing their scouting.

Their area was around the lake.

The dockyards showed no activity.

They'd checked out the smaller fishing village and found it seemed to be completely abandoned. Ruby commented on that, saying that earlier she'd seen Marauders there. David theorized that they'd probably been pulled to be part of the group to take back the fort.

After that they'd carefully checked out the fishing village from afar, and Ruby again commented that there seemed to be practically a skeleton crew of Marauders. David studied them with a pair of binoculars he'd picked up from the military stash. They looked angry, fidgety, and on edge. The fishers were watching them closely, he noticed.

Good. They would strike when the time was right. After that, they had ambushed a squad of Marauders in the woods as they moved further down the road, hoping to get a look at the north side of the lake.

David had very nearly gotten his head blown off doing that, but overall it had been a success. Ruby was quicker on her feet than he was, and a better shot. They'd gotten as close as they could to the north side of the lake, which was to say not too close at all, and studied it as much as they could. There didn't seem to be any Marauder activity over there.

He could see no boats on the water. And he didn't see any activity near the far side of the lake, where hopefully Helen was still helping his friends rest, recover, and get to safety.

They'd ended up continuing along to do some additional scouting, heading towards Jennifer's old house north of the abandoned hospital. They found it raided, the place ransacked and tossed, a lot of stuff missing, and David was glad that Jennifer had long since moved her most important stuff over to Haven, to her new basement dwelling.

It still pissed him off, though. They moved on to the watchtower where he'd set up that cache and took a break there, grabbing a bite to eat and taking a half-hour rest. Finally, they'd gotten back to it.

The last of their scouting brought them north of the woods, to the trailers where he had initially found Lindsay's group. There had been a small Marauder presence there, but judging by the fact that they hadn't seemed to be doing much, and had been caught completely off guard, and that they were put down with relative ease, he had the notion that maybe they'd stumbled upon a group of slackers looking for a place to hide out for a while and duck work. Or duck maybe getting killed by the locals. Sad for them.

Once they'd made sure they had gotten them all, he and Ruby had gathered up whatever resources they could from them, (they weren't well-equipped and he had to wonder if they were outcasts among the Marauders), then they had finally made for the hospital. By the time they got to the place, it was almost dawn. The first rays of sunshine were just barely beginning to become visible over the horizon.

David felt a deep weariness settling on him and knew he was going to need to take some kind of a break.

"Think it's clear?" Ruby murmured quietly as they approached the abandoned hospital.

"No way to be sure, let's go in through the back, quietly," he replied.

She nodded and they made their way through the woods, past trees and bushes, careful to make as little noise as possible. He didn't hear anything, and the

Marauders didn't seem to be known for being quiet, but assumptions were dangerous in situations like these. Ruby went first, as she was quicker and quieter than him, and he watched her back. He noticed her tail was completely still and down flat against one of her legs.

They slipped in through the back and cleared the room there, closing the door quietly behind them, then pressed on. The main room was just as empty as it was before, the blood dried now. They'd ended up dragging the bodies out before leaving, hiding them among the foliage. They checked the side room, the kitchen area, and then moved up to the second story, cleared it, found nothing waiting for them there, nor in the big open attic that was the third story that David had only seen a few times, then returned to the second story.

"Now what?" Ruby murmured.

"Now we wait," he replied, and sat down heavily in a nearby chair.

They had come to one of the patient rooms, which looked like it had once been a large bathroom. Where the tub might have been there was now a bed. There was still a simple shower stall in the corner, though David doubted it worked at all. There was also what might once have been a fancy counter with a pair of sinks built into it. It was pretty clean, like the rest of the room. Well, all things considered. It was hard to get a place that was totally clean in this world.

Ruby leaned against the counter. She looked tired, her fur sticking up in several places, matted with blood and mud. Her long arms of lean muscle were folded across her chest, and he had to admit she still looked really damned good in her sleeveless vest and cargo shorts. She noticed him looking at her and he saw one eyebrow raise.

"David..." she said, uncertainly.

"Yeah?" he replied, then yawned and covered his mouth. "Sorry," he murmured.

"No, it's fine. I'm tired, too. I was going to ask..." She hesitated again, looked away. He heard a steady thump and realized that her tail was beginning to twitch. "Maybe I shouldn't."

"Whatever it is, you might as well ask now. It's not like I'll get mad at you if the answer is no," he replied.

She sighed. "I suppose you are right. I'm bad at predicting people's reactions to things. But I trust you." She seemed to steel herself slightly. "We made love a while ago. And I really enjoyed it. I thought I'd like to try it again, with you. And that's something that's come up in my mind several times since all this started. I could die. And I guess I want to enjoy it again, once more, just in case. And now seemed like a good opportunity."

"Oh...yeah, I'd love to," he replied, getting to his feet. "Why did you think I would be angry or reject you?"

"Well, besides the usual reasons, I was worried that you might be offended. Your loved ones are captured or possibly injured out there, and here I am trying to waste time with sex..."

"It isn't a waste of time, Ruby," he said, walking over to her. He settled his hands on her slim hips, looked up into her cat eyes. Good lord, she was tall. He'd forgotten that she had a solid four inches of height on him. "It's not like we'd be doing anything else."

"We could be resting," she murmured.

He laughed. "Fair point, but I need some damned

stress relief."

"Me too. Can we do it right here?"

"What, on the counter?"

"Yeah. I know there's a bed in the corner but I've always wanted to do it on the counter like this. I've read about that in books...it always seems so intense."

"Yes, we can do it on the counter, it's at just the right height for fucking," he replied, and then he gently slipped his hand over the back of her neck and slowly began to guide her face down towards his own.

She let him, leaning down, and their lips met. He groaned and closed his eyes. Kissing a woman was, in that moment, such an intense pleasure, a release. Just feeling her against him. His time with Azure and then Catalina already felt like it had happened over a week ago, somehow. That raging lust was back again.

He began tugging at her clothes, and unzipped her vest. She let him get it off of her as they made out, twisting and twining tongues together, tasting each other. Enjoying each other. She was just wearing a sports bra beneath the vest and they broke the kiss for the barest time it took to get it off, over her head. It caught on one of her cat ears and she laughed softly, flicked it, and tossed the bra aside.

David cupped her bare, furred, firm breasts. As he began unbuttoning her shorts, he had to admit that there was a part of him that felt guilty over this. But he was too tired to focus on that, and pushing it away was easier this time.

For now, he just wanted to lose himself in Ruby, in her long, lean, furry body. They had a really nice rhythm going with the kissing, and he could tell by her body language that she needed this as much as he did, and that she'd missed him as much as he'd missed her. He got her pants undone and she let them drop, which they did, easily, as her pockets were weighed down with magazines and other useful gear.

She took her panties down and then hopped up on the counter.

"I'm ready," she said, opening her legs.

"You want me to do anything with my mouth? I will," he said as he hastily shed his tactical gear, leaving just his shirt and pants.

She smiled. "I appreciate it, but I really just want sex right now. I'm wet enough."

"Okay then."

He dug his cock out of his pants and stepped up to the counter and to her. He was right: it was perfect for fucking height. Wanting to lose himself inside of her, he began working his way into her. She let out a soft gasp and he looked up, into her eyes. She stared back, her own eyes wide and intense as he carefully worked his way into her.

"You *are* wet," he murmured.

"Ah! Yes...oh my...you are as big as I remember," she murmured, spreading her legs out a little wider and readjusting herself slightly to give him easier access.

"I'll be careful," he replied, and then he kissed her again.

She slipped her arms across his back, holding him to her as he carefully worked his way into her, slowly making love with her, feeling that tight, wet perfection. One of her hands came up higher and he felt her run her fingers through his hair and he shuddered in response to it.

One of his hands went up and cupped one of her high, firm breasts again, groping it as he got all the way inside of her. And once he was comfortably into her, David began to stroke smoothly in and out of her, sliding his rigid cock into that sweet, tight, wet pussy of hers over and over again, not going too fast or too hard.

She moaned quietly and kissed him harder as they fucked.

Ruby had always been a bit of an enigma to him. She seemed curiously detached, not just from him, but from everyone. She had friends, she liked people, he knew that, but he had the idea that she didn't quite experience those connections the same way most other people did. Although he didn't know if he was actually right, or if she just chose to respond to her connections differently. Maybe she took longer to warm up to people, or preferred to keep some distance between herself and everyone else. Or maybe that just happened naturally for her.

But he felt connected with her right now, and he didn't know if it was because she was opening up to him, or because she was particularly vulnerable given all that had happened, or something else entirely. All he knew was that he enjoyed the connection he was feeling with her. He enjoyed everything about the experience.

The way she was panting, the way she closed her eyes, the way she grabbed at him, the way she tilted her head slightly to deepen the kiss.

"Take your shirt off," she whispered.

He complied immediately, his pants had already fallen down around his ankles. He tossed his shirt aside and she immediately hugged him to her. The wonderful soft caress of her fur against his bare skin reinvigorated him.

David continued driving into her, going a bit harder and faster now, as she began asking for that with her body, almost demanding it. She grunted and moaned, having to keep it quiet given their situation, as he screwed her. And suddenly she went rigid, her whole body tensing up, and she let out a strangled sound and began to come.

"Oh fuck, Ruby..." he groaned, gritting his teeth as he continued pounding his cock into that fantastically wet, convulsing inhuman vagina.

He started letting off almost immediately.

They came together, locked in sexual union and shared bliss, leaning against each other, resting their foreheads together, trembling and shaking with the orgasm. The pleasure rolled smoothly through his body, magnified by Ruby's own orgasm, and he was briefly transported from this world of pain and fear and suffering.

Only briefly, though.

He came back to himself, and when he did, he had the awareness, somehow, that there was someone in the building with them. Ruby could sense it too, he could tell. Pulling out of her and turning away from her, he walked over to the table where he'd set his gear down and snatched up his pistol.

Stupid, he should've had it with him. Again, this was the problem with pushing yourself (and okay yeah, getting distracted by hot sex): he got sloppy and distracted and slow. Naked save for his boots, he aimed at the door.

A sound came, the creaking of the stairs, and he tensed.

"David...it's just me," came a familiar voice.

Relief flooded him. "Goddamnit, Akila," he said, lowering the pistol. "You scared the fucking shit out of us."

"Hey, I *could* have just came and stood in the

doorway while you were fucking," she replied, her voice getting closer.

"That's a really good way to get shot," Ruby said.

"Which is exactly why I didn't do that," she replied. She appeared in the doorway. "Ah, I thought it might be you he was nailing. I heard you two fucking and got drawn in. You're noisy."

"We were being quiet," David said as he set the pistol down and began the process of pulling his clothes and then his tactical gear back on.

"Not to me you weren't," she replied.

David studied her. She looked practically the same as when he'd first seen her when she'd saved their asses near the bunker. Maybe a bit dirtier, more tired, with a bit more gear. But she looked as lethal and sexy as ever.

"I'm assuming that huge explosion earlier was you?" she asked.

"Yeah, we blew up Lima Company's old fort," David replied.

She hesitated, her eyebrows raising. "...completely?"

"Yes. It's completely wiped off the map, and we probably took a good seventy or eighty down, though a lot of them were Lima Company. They're probably just about wiped out now."

"Shit, what else have you been up to?"

"We rescued Val and some of her people, tracked down Azure and she's in on this now, and assaulted the dockyards and rescued the remains of Lima Company who actually weren't down with, you know, enslaving an entire region. And we killed a bunch of Marauder assholes in between those things," he replied.

"I'm impressed, but not surprised. Where's Evie? Where are the others?"

"I've been sending people to the island through the mining tunnel," he replied. "Evie's there. So are several others. Katya's there. And April."

"Huh...okay, yeah, that's a great idea, actually." She smiled suddenly. "I *knew* you were something special when I met you. You and Cait and Ellie. You have survival instincts that most non-nymphs don't."

"Thanks...what have *you* been up to?" he asked.

She shrugged. "Killing Marauders. Staying alive. Catching a few hours of sleep and a meal when I can find a quiet place. It's interesting. In a way, those long weeks of isolation and survival before we formally met were the worst of my life by far. But in another way, I enjoyed them in a grim sort of way. Relying completely on myself, knowing for a fact that no one would come help me. It was frightening, but there was a bleak comfort in that certainty.

"I kind of disappeared into myself, becoming a huntress, a killer, a tool. That's what the past few days have been like, only this time, I know that I have friends and lovers around. That when this is over...provided all goes well, I'll have them to go back to. It makes it much less bleak."

"Well, as much as I can understand that, I'm afraid I must insist that your time being a killer huntress in the woods be finished. We need you now," David said.

"Oh? You're ready for a final assault?" she asked.

"I think so, but I won't know until the others get here. We've been scouting all over the region for the past few hours. Why don't you tell me what you think of the Marauder forces at present?" he suggested.

"They're definitely hurting," she said. "I couldn't go half an hour without at least hearing or seeing a squad moving through the woods twenty four hours ago. Now I can go a solid two hours moving around without finding anything. I know some of it is me. I've killed a good fifty or sixty of them since last we spoke."

"That's impressive," Ruby murmured.

"I'm very good at murder," Akila replied. He noticed that she didn't seem proud of that, but she also didn't seem ashamed of it, either.

"Evidently. I'm glad you're on our side," David said.

Akila shrugged. "You may be right, if the others say something similar, that the time has come to push them out before they get a chance to get backup."

He sighed. "Yeah. That's why I want to keep pushing."

"When will the others get here?" Akila asked.

"Soon," he replied. Then paused. "Hopefully."

...

They started showing up ten minutes later.

It was a stressful hour. Each time someone else showed up, they all tensed, wondering if it was the Marauders coming for them. But each time it was some of his friends. They all showed up a little worse for the wear: tired, dirty, in some cases injured, but thankfully none seriously. Finally, when the last of them showed up, Ellie and Ashley, they all convened and began sharing what they had learned. David listened carefully as they told him what they had seen, spread out all over the region. He processed all this information, then took a quick walk around in the downstairs of the hospital, mulling over it.

Finally, he came back up, finding everyone sitting down, drinking from whatever they had gotten their hands on or eating anything they had found, mostly from cans, or tending to wounds. Catalina had already fallen asleep. Match nudged her gently with his foot as David came in, and slowly they all got to their feet.

"What's the plan, boss?" Val asked.

David looked at her. "*You* are calling *me* boss?"

She shrugged. "Yeah, you pretty much are. I can recognize a leader when I see one, and know that I'm not one. So what's the plan?" she asked.

"From what I've heard, the Marauders are hurting. I think we've been able to kill two thirds of them through our tactics, maybe even as much as three quarters of their entire force. They don't have enough for patrols, and at this point they may even have pulled their forces back to the four settlements. In this case, the time has come to make the last push. I know for a fact that Thatch and his people will be there for us if we need them and let them know the time has come. Ruby? What about your people?" he asked.

"They'll fight," she replied simply.

"Okay, good." He yawned, rubbed his eyes, refocused. "Akila, you're the best tracker among us. Can you find Vanessa?"

"Yes," she replied.

"Within an hour?"

"Yes."

"Half an hour?"

"Almost certainly."

"You sound pretty confident," Ellie murmured.

"I am," she replied simply.

"Okay, that's your job. Ruby, get with Akila and establish a meeting point near the fishing village. Ruby, you will go there and wait, scouting out the situation and figuring out the best way to make an assault. Akila, you will find Vanessa and if she is still in fighting shape, convince her to help you make the assault on the fishing village. The three of you will take it as quickly as possible."

He turned. "Ellie, I want you to take Ashley and Cole and mount an assault on the farms. Thatch and his people *should* provide help from the inside. Again, take control as fast as you can. Now, Catalina, Tennyson, Match, Val, and Azure, you're all with me. We're going to make an assault on Haven. Same thing should happen: our people should be ready to take advantage of the situation and start killing from the inside.

"Once we have secured all three of these locations, we are going to arm and mobilize as many people as possible and hit the middle settlement with everything we've got. As many people as possible. That seems to be where they're headquartered. And, ideally, we'll wipe them out and get our people and our homes back. Now...get ready with your watches. I'm going to give us an hour from now to get into position. I want us to launch our attacks as simultaneously as possible..."

They all began to sync watches, and once that was done, they started to get ready for what might be the most difficult battle of their lives.

CHAPTER THIRTEEN

David wasn't sure he had ever taken such a huge gamble in his entire life.

He had played dice with his life before. Dozens, probably hundreds of times at this point. So far, he'd always won. Technically speaking. And by now, he'd been forced to play dice with other people's lives, too. That always felt a million times worse. It was one thing to fuck up and the consequences were on *your* head. It was a completely different thing to fuck up and the consequences were delivered to another.

This was to be the final gambit, if it went the way it was supposed to.

He was leading five people to assault a village.

Granted, two of them were absolutely certified hardcore warriors and the rest were at least decently trained soldiers, and he was pretty confident of his own abilities, but if his people at Haven didn't rise up, then there wasn't going to be much of a battle.

From the recon report Ellie and Ashley had given when they'd looked at Haven, it seemed like his people weren't chained up or anything. That might've changed though. If it had, this was going to get bad quick. They were mostly in the main square, under guard, doing stuff.

Sorting supplies, repairing weapons or clothes or armor or gear, preparing meals, skinning animals or gutting fish, chopping firewood.

Basically what they'd be doing otherwise, but under guard and no doubt to an unreasonable level. David assumed they were pushing his people as hard as they possibly could without outright breaking them. An exhausted populace was easier to control.

He was counting on fury and adrenaline to help them.

This was also going to be a more difficult battle because they couldn't just slaughter indiscriminately, not like at the dockyards or the fort. Not only were his people in there, but that was their home. It needed to still be there after this.

They were over the river now. The sun was up, though it was still early enough in the morning that mist clung to everything, giving the area an eerie, ominous vibe. They were maybe five minutes out from Haven. Already, he could hear the sounds of work coming from up ahead. He had been considering the way to do this and none of it was looking too great. They were all great shots, but there'd be no sniper support this time. He'd considered having Azure hang back with a scoped rifle and do the job, but she was just too useful on the front lines. So they were going to pull a rather risky maneuver.

As they came within sight of Haven, David held up a fist and dropped to one knee while turning around to face the others.

They quickly gathered around him.

He studied them for just a second before speaking. They all looked the same, all looked like he looked no doubt: tired, dirty, angry, grim. Ready for war. Even Azure was looking noticeably worse for the wear by now.

"Azure, you're with me. We're going to assault the front gate. Val, think you can manage by yourself?" he asked.

She held up the rifle she'd picked up. She switched to a scoped burst-fire rifle at some point during all this. It looked very accurate and lethal in her grasp. "Yes," she said. "I can handle whatever you throw at me."

"Okay. I want you to attack from the right. Ellie said there's holes in the fence now. Try to get in if you can before launching the assault, you should be relatively out of sight. Tennyson, Match, Catalina, head for the left side. There's a back entrance there. It'll probably be guarded. Take out the guards and get inside when the shooting starts." He paused, looked at them all more intently, his expression growing no doubt grimmer. "You *must* be careful. Besides the fact that we need Haven mostly intact, what matters about a billion times more is that there are *our* people in there. Causalities on our side are *unacceptable,* do you understand?"

They all nodded, their expressions grave.

"Good. Split up. We've got four minutes to get into position and get ready. Val, if you can, slip in in three minutes, but wait for mine and Azure's assault. Good luck."

They split off and headed for their designated locations.

David and Azure hurried over to the dense collection of trees that sat in front of Haven, stopping about twenty yards short of it. He'd always considered trimming back this part of the forest, or at least clearing it out a bit, but he never had, because somewhere, in the back of his head, he'd always wondered if something like this might happen. His people knew what to look for from the watchtowers, they knew this place like the back of their hand by now, they knew the likeliest hiding spots. The Marauders wouldn't, not yet.

And they were going to suffer for that.

He brought Azure to a location that would give them a decent view of the watchtowers that they'd assembled at the front gate of Haven, but kept them relatively obscured. He saw a pair of Marauders in each tower, each armed with a rifle.

"We're going to have to take all four of them out really fast," David whispered. He checked his way, not much time left now. "Can you do that?"

"Yes," Azure replied confidently.

"Okay. You take the two on the left, I'll take the two on the right, then I'll make a break for the gate and you shoot any you can see. Once I'm up there, I'll cover you and you come up. Then we head in and wipe them out."

"Got it," she said.

David kept his eyes on his watch. They had to start these assaults at roughly the same time, not just here at Haven, but across the region. When there were only thirty seconds left, he got into position and took aim on the first guard on the right. Counting down slowly in his head, when he got to ten seconds, he made final preparations for the assault. This was it. Moment of truth. The time in his head finished counting down and he squeezed the trigger.

It was a perfect headshot.

As fast as he could, the precise moment he saw the bullet connect, he snapped to the next target and fired. Azure had fired in tandem with him.

Four bullets went out, four living people became corpses.

One of them toppled over the edge of the watchtower, fell a little ways, and became caught on the top of the fence. David kept his rifle out as he rose to his feet and began making his way towards the front gate, hustling across the open space. People were yelling and he could hear gunfire from the left.

A Marauder rushed down the little road that led

up to the main gate and David fired three times, managing to catch her in the neck and drop her. As he reached the main entrance, more Marauders appeared, and he could hear gunfire coming from the right now. Val was getting to it. He carefully aimed and fired, scoring a headshot and downing one of them, then dropped to one knee as another two returned fire.

Azure had to be running for his position by now. He kept firing, pouring all his attention into the now three Marauders that were in the central path now, making for the cover of the cabins as they fired at him. He shot one through the leg and sent him crashing to the ground, then put four rounds into another's chest.

At least one of them went through as he saw a spray of blood come out. Then a round punched him in the chest and he fell back on his ass. Azure appeared at his side, firing with her own rifle. She popped off eight shots while he got back to his feet.

"You okay?" she asked.

"Fine," he replied. "Let's go!"

The front gate wasn't locked or secured, so they must have been getting ready to go out for the day, (no doubt they escorted groups of his people to the rabbit and fish traps). He got it open and stepped inside, Azure right behind him. It was chaos now. He heard shouting, screaming, gunfire, doors being kicked open, glass shattering, someone was crying, what might've been a kid. Fuck, they had to get this over with very fast.

They shifted to the right side of the initial road that led into the central area of Haven. As they moved along the first cabin there, David stepped out around the corner to clear it and found himself looking at a Marauder wielding a shotgun.

Aimed right at him.

The world exploded.

Something kicked him in the chest like a cannon going off and then the air was blown out of him as pain erupted inside of him. He was physically thrown off his feet and slammed into the ground on his back, sending yet another wave of solid pain. He heard Azure scream his name, then gunfire and pained yelling, and then more gunfire. Suddenly he was being dragged. Everything was dark and hazy and off-kilter.

Slowly, his breath came back into his abused lungs.

"David! David, please be okay," Azure said, appearing in his field of vision. She looked around furtively, panic written in her normally serene features.

"Fine," he wheezed. Gritting his teeth, he looked down at his chest. He expected to see blood, a fountain of it, but impossibly, it looked like the tactical gear had held up. "Holy shit," he gasped, desperately trying to draw breath.

"I think it stopped the shot," she whispered.

"Go," he said. She hesitated, a look of uncertainty on her face. David drew a deeper breath. "*Go,*" he said more firmly. "You have to help them. I'll be fine."

She stared at him, torn, and then nodded tightly. "I'll kill them all," she said, then got to her feet and rushed off.

David took the barest amount of time he could get away with before struggling back up to his feet. He looked around and then stumbled back over to the entrance to the little alleyway created between the two cabins where Azure had dragged him. It was still chaos out there, but it sounded somehow more controlled, and there was a lot of yelling going on. Angry yelling. Righteous yelling. 'It's-time-for-payback' yelling.

His people were rising up.

He spied his rifle, snagged it, and lurched towards the main conflict. He saw a lot of his people in their regular clothes fighting with the Marauders now. David saw a Marauder kick one of his people to the ground and raise a pistol to finish him off. He shot the Marauder in the head. The man on the ground snagged the dead Marauder's pistol, surged to his feet, turned and put five shots into the back of nearby Marauder with a shotgun.

A dozen similar scenes of chaos were playing out all around him as he came into the central area, his chest still screaming in agony. Had he broken something? There was too much general pain to be able to tell. Either way, he could keep going for now, that was all that mattered. Fuck, that had been *way* too close.

David quickly began picking out targets of surviving Marauders, who were beginning to get the idea that they were fucked, and trying to flee. He shot two men in the back and didn't feel particularly bad about it, not at this point. Already, he could see that they had managed to kill at least one or two of his people.

He recognized one guy from Robert's initial group, a pale man who'd mostly kept to himself but was a pretty hard worker, somewhere in his late forties. Richard had been his name. Now he was dead, a hole in his forehead, his brains leaking out onto the ground of the place that he had finally called home. No, David didn't feel particularly bad about murdering the fucking assholes who had unnecessarily *forced* this on them all, and who had completely brought this on themselves.

Finally, the gunfire fell away as the last of the Marauders were put down. He looked around, trying to pick faces out of the crowd. There was Lindsay, looking grim and furious, blood sprayed across the front of her shirt and onto her neck, none of it hers, though, he quickly realized. He also saw Robert, crouched over someone who'd been shot, helping them with a few others, his actions quick and decisive. And Jennifer.

There was Jennifer. She was comforting someone now that it was over.

David hurried over to her, passing Azure on the way, who was in the process of gathering weapons and getting them into the hands of the more able-bodied survivors.

"Jennifer!" he wheezed.

Her eyes widened as she looked up. "David!" she said. She gave the person she was talking to a soft pat. "I'll be right back," she said.

"Go, I'll be okay," the woman murmured.

He and Jennifer met out in front of the main office and hugged tightly.

"Oh my God, I thought you were dead," she whispered, trembling. "Oh my God, David. They were saying that they'd finally got you in that huge explosion."

He laughed, then groaned. "Of course they'd try to spin it their way. *We* set that damned explosion off. Killed most of Lima Company and blew up their base."

She frowned, pulling back. "Lima Company...what? You *killed* them?"

"They betrayed us, Jennifer," he said. "The Marauders came to them before all this and they *agreed* to help them enslave us. Not all of them. Catalina turned against them. So did Cole and a few others. But listen, we don't have time to catch up. I need your help. This is the final assault. We *have* to get to the new settlement now so we can attack it and kill the Marauders once and for all."

Jennifer's expression hardened and she nodded. "I understand. Let me find some gear and I'll be ready."

"Good. I–"

"David!" Azure yelled.

She sounded worried. He turned around, saw her crouched over someone laying on the ground. A large, bulky someone.

"Crap," he growled and jogged off.

Val was down for the count. He immediately saw the problem as he approached: she'd been shot in the gut.

Twice.

And once in the shoulder.

"Of *fucking* course I'd be the one to get shot," she growled as he crouched by her. She hawked and spat some blood onto the ground. "Just lemme get patched up and I'll be ready to help you keep kicking ass."

"Val, you're staying here," he said flatly.

"Fuck off! I'm not staying here–"

He shook his head and put a hand on her undamaged shoulder. "Val. You are staying here. You're too much of a liability." He paused. "Besides, I need someone I can trust here to watch over the wounded and the young in case more Marauders show up."

She stared angrily up at him, then sighed heavily and looked away, out over the others. There were two dozen people moving around, half of them wounded in one way or another. Mostly they were simple wounds, but they would require attention.

"Fine," she said.

He realized some people had approached him. He glanced over his shoulder as he dug into his pack for some medical supplies. Jennifer, Robert, and Lindsay had come over. He was extremely grateful to see them. In a way, he had been intending to pass the torch of leadership of Haven to them after moving to the new settlement. They'd always stepped up and helped out in one way or another, often being team leaders in several different situations.

"Is she going to be okay?" Robert asked.

"I'll be fine," Val grunted.

"I'll need someone who knows a bit more to help her," David said as he got the supplies out and set them down beside her.

"I can handle it," Val muttered as she worked at stopping the bleeding.

"I can do it," Lindsay said, crouching beside her and taking over the job.

"Good. Okay people, I know this is abrupt, but we're going to need your help. This is just phase one of the plan. We have to mount a larger assault on the central settlement," David said.

"What about the farm? The fishing village? Lima Company?" Robert asked.

"Ellie, Akila, Ashley, and others are mounting their own assaults on the farm and the fishing village. Lima Company's out of the picture. We're going to all hit the central settlement at once...ideally," David explained. He looked at Azure. "Take the soldiers and go get into position ahead of us. I'll gather whoever I can, okay?"

"On it," she replied, and rushed off. He looked after her. Fuck, he hadn't even had a chance to see if Catalina and the others were still alive. But he saw them, three uniform-wearing figures, still upright and moving around.

He looked back at the others. "Lindsay, finish up with Val. Robert, Jennifer, with me. We're going to find every able-bodied person who can fight, and arm and mobilize them. Lindsay, join us when you can, and let's fucking finish this."

...

Between himself, Jennifer, Robert, Lindsay, and the others they had gathered who were in fighting shape, they had managed to get a dozen altogether. Which meant they were going to assault the central settlement with just sixteen people. Not great, but not terrible. And the others were going to help too, hopefully. That number would hopefully triple once the other settlements had been overthrown and were coming their way.

David had been forced to take a little break, as the pain in his chest was starting to bother him. He'd finally taken off his gear and had Lindsay check him over. There was a nasty bruise, a big one, in the center of his chest, but after taking a more in-depth look at him, she said he likely was okay.

No broken or cracked ribs, anyway.

After taking some painkillers, he'd gotten his shit together, grabbed whatever ammo he could, and finally gathered the people up and led them out of Haven.

He couldn't hear any fighting anywhere else, which was either very good or very bad. Either way, he simply couldn't waste any time or any people going to check. He was just going to have to trust that things had turned out for the best.

At the moment, he was looking for Azure and the others. David had fucked up: he hadn't set a meeting point. Again, the consequences of operating on the fly with too little sleep and too much pain and strain. But luck found him: he only wasted about two minutes hunting through the forest before tracking the four of them down squatting among the trees. As he approached them, Catalina turned to look back at him.

He hesitated on approach.

Something in her expression told him something was deeply, deeply wrong.

"David," Azure murmured, turning around, "we have a problem."

"What?" he asked, his heart starting to thunder in his chest again, the pit of his stomach freezing and then dropping away. She waved him forward. He joined her and pulled out his binoculars. Putting them to his eyes, he nearly panicked right then and there.

Near the center of the settlement were two figures, tied to wooden poles driven into the ground, surrounded by a dozen dark-clad figures.

Cait and Lara.

"Jesus fucking shit," he whispered. "Aw *shit.*"

"What is it?" Lindsay hissed. "What's wrong?"

"They've got Cait and Lara tied up down there," he said, forcing himself to calm down. He was going to be no good to anyone if he panicked. "Goddamnit, where the fuck are the others?" he growled, looking to the left, then to the right.

Still nothing on either side.

"What are we going to do?" Jennifer asked.

He set the binoculars aside and took off his backpack. "I'm going down there."

"What? No," Azure replied immediately.

"I need to buy some time, maybe try some kind of BS negotiation tactic," he replied, setting his guns aside. He passed the rifle to Robert, who took it reluctantly.

"David, you cannot–" Azure began, but he turned to look at her so fast she hesitated and sat back slightly.

"Azure, and this goes for all of you, *whatever happens, you fucking save Cait and Lara*. Do you understand me? Save them, and save everyone else down there. *Whatever happens*." He paused, looked around. "Do you *understand?*" he asked firmly.

"Yes," Azure murmured. "Just...do not die down there."

"I fully intend to survive this encounter, but if it's a choice between me or Cait or Lara or anyone else for that matter, I'll put my own ass on the line first. Okay." He stood up as he tossed the last of his gear away, just wearing his tactical armor now. "The best shots among you, get scoped rifles and get into position. I want you to open fire and take out everyone near Cait and Lara once I give you the signal. The signal is my raising my right hand. Got it?"

"Got it," Azure said.

He took a deep breath, let it out slowly. "God fucking help me."

"Good luck," Robert said, and the others murmured similar things.

David nodded. "And you."

He shifted about fifty yards to the left of their

current position, as not to give them away, and came out from that direction. He walked out of the woods slowly but steadily, moving towards the settlement.

There were a *lot* of Marauders there. Maybe eighty of them in total, all of them armed and armored with that black leather they wore. It was tough stuff. He'd hardly gone ten feet before the perimeter guards had him covered with rifles as he approached. They might not realize who he was and kill him. Or they might realize who he was and kill him. But they had to want him to come to them, because the threat was obviously meant for him, or at the very least for the leadership of Haven. He wondered how much they knew about him at this point.

"Hands up!" one of the guards shouted as he approached the perimeter fence they'd managed to establish before all this shit went down.

David put his hands up. "Looking to talk to whoever's in charge."

"Shut up. Get over here, nice and slow," the guard replied.

David walked over. As soon as they did, one covered him by pressing the barrel of a pistol to his skull while the other patted him down.

"What's your name?" the one patting him down growled.

"David."

"Shit, he's the one she wants to talk to," he muttered.

"Back up with that pistol," David said.

"Fuck you," the man snapped and shoved it harder against his head.

David turned to look at him. He was exhausted, enraged, and convinced that he had at least some level of protection. They weren't going to kill him.

"Get that pistol out of my face or I'll kill you," he said calmly.

"Fuck you! Shut the fuck up!" the man snapped.

The pistol disappeared for a second, only to be replaced by a fist smashing into his jaw. Stars exploded and washed across his vision as he staggered and a fresh wave of pain hit him.

"Goddamnit! She said not to hurt him you dumbshit!" the other guard snapped.

"You heard what he said! Fuck him!" the first one growled.

David straightened back up and spit a mouthful of blood out. "Well, I warned you," he said.

"You aren't gonna do shit, you fucking pussy," the first guard snarled, and shoved the pistol back in his face.

The second he did, David's hands came up like lightning. He snatched the pistol out of the man's hand, twisting it to break his grip, brought it around, put the barrel against his forehead and squeezed the trigger.

"*FUCK!*" the other guard screamed. He raised his own pistol and put it to David's head. "Drop it! Now! *Drop it!*" he screamed.

David dropped the pistol. "I warned him," he replied. He looked at the surviving guard. "You heard me warn him. I told him right to his face."

"Goddamnit!" the guard snapped, covering him with the pistol.

David turned fully to face him. He heard running footsteps. "You know what's gonna happen if you don't get that pistol out of my face, right?"

"Fuck!" the surviving guard hissed, and lowered the pistol.

"What the hell is going on here?!" someone demanded as the gate was thrown open.

"He shot Peter! He shot him in the face!" the other guard yelled.

"Jesus fuck-you didn't fucking think to pat him down?!"

"He took Peter's gun right out of his hands and shot him!"

"I warned him first," David said, looking at the man who seemed to be the leader of this other group that had come over. "I told him right to his face, if he didn't get that gun out of my face I was going to kill him. He didn't listen."

"Jesus fucking Christ, if she didn't want you alive..." the big man growled.

"Stop talking and take me to her then," David replied.

The man, who was almost the same size and shape as Val, began to turn red in the face. Then he reached out, grabbed David by the front of his tactical gear, and yanked him almost off his feet.

"Walk!" he screamed once he'd pulled him through the gate and aimed him towards the place where they had Cait and Lara tied up.

"None of you are getting out of here alive," David said.

"Shut up!" the big man snapped, shoving him.

David had to resist the suddenly overwhelming urge to turn around and punch the man in the throat. But he was focused on Cait and Lara now. They were both staring intently at him now. They were walking down the central road between the various sections of the settlement.

It was obvious that the Marauders were intent on continuing the work he and the others had done getting the place set up. Though thankfully they hadn't gotten that far into it. The assault, if it was still going to happen, had a decent chance of succeeding.

Cait and Lara were in basically the center of the settlement, right in the middle of the road that cut through it.

A dozen guards ringed them, and a tall woman in a black uniform, different from the leather armor, stood within that ring, ahead of Cait and Lara, with her arms clasped behind her back. She reminded him of Stern.

In fact...

"You sick fuck," David said, realizing that one of the men guarding them was, in fact, Stern himself.

"If I didn't have strict orders not to," Stern said, leaning forward a little, his eyes wide and full of fury beyond anything David had ever seen in him before, "I'd be punching your skull into paste right about now."

"You'd certainly be *trying* to, little man," David replied.

Stern clenched his jaw and straightened back up immediately. No doubt he had just come dangerously close to smashing David's face in.

Good, the more of them that were pissed the better.

Pissed meant mistakes, which he might actually be making right now, given how enraged he was. He looked at Cait and Lara.

"Come closer," the tall woman said.

She had a firm but oddly friendly voice. As David stepped through the ring of guards, he realized that it wasn't friendliness on her face. Not even close. Smug superiority.

It was funny how many times he'd seen

something like that in the women he loved, that little bit of smugness that usually came from successfully enticing him into something. Now he just hated it and he wanted to smash this woman's face in.

Her skin was ashen, very pale, and he was surprised to realize that he could see her veins, faintly. She was a wraith.

"So, you're David," she said, her hands still behind her back. "You've caused quite a lot of trouble, though that was clearly the point." She paused. "You know, I've led ten campaigns like this. So far, this one has caused the most trouble by far. You and your friends are absolutely something else. We get fighters and we get rebellions and resistance movements, sometimes we get hardcore killers like you. But usually...the hardcore killers are the first to sign up.

"What makes you so different? *No one* here has willing surrendered themselves...besides your military friends, of course. We had to force the issue with everyone else. Stern here told me we'd have to. Turns out he was right. So what's so special about you, David? What makes you different?"

"I'm not a fucking monster," he replied. Then he turned to look at Cait, who had been staring at him the whole time, tears in her eyes.

Whatever happened, however things turned out, he needed to say this at least once.

"Cait, I love you."

"I love you too, David," she replied, and he was so grateful to hear a lot of strength in her voice. He held her eyes a bit longer, then looked at Lara.

"Lara, I love you."

She swallowed, and the expression she had been holding, one of flat rage, broke briefly. "I love you too, David," she replied quietly.

He turned his attention back to the woman.

"Interesting," she murmured.

"What do you want?" he asked. "They keep saying you want to talk to me."

"Yes, I do," she agreed. "I want to offer you a job. I was going to just kill you at first, as I thought you were too dangerous to let live, but then I realized you were too useful to kill. So, this is my offer: swear loyalty to me, convince your killer friends to join me, and I will install you as my right-hand man. You'll have access to whatever you want, whatever you need. You'll kill our enemies, and bring more lands in our empire." She paused. "If you decline my offer, I'll execute you and your pretty pregnant redhead and all your other friends. It's only a matter of time before it happens." She paused again, studied him closely.

"So, what's it going to be?" she asked.

"I have a counteroffer," David replied. "Take all your 'friends' and get the fuck out of my region and never, *ever* come back, or I'll kill every last one of you motherfuckers."

A small smile came onto the woman's pallid face. Her hands at last came out from behind her back. "It's going to be a shame to kill you. You've proven exceptionally resourceful, with, simply put, amazing endurance and luck."

She held a large, wicked-looking serrated blade in her hand.

"Remember," David said. He pointed at her, making her hesitate. "I gave you a chance. I'll give you one more...cut them free and walk away or I'll kill you right now."

She laughed. "I saw what you did to my man at the gate. It won't work on me. I'm faster than you are and–"

David interrupted her. "Okay, I warned you. That was it. That was your last chance."

A hateful, ugly look came onto her face as she hefted the knife. "I'm going to enjoy this."

"No, you won't," he replied, and raised his arm.

Immediately, a rifle cracked and a hole opened up on her forehead. She just had time to make a very surprised expression before collapsing in a heap. At the same time, David saw Lara, who had apparently been working her bindings to get herself out of them while they were talking, free herself and leap away from the post.

More rifles fired.

Three of the guards around them fell. David rushed at Stern, who was already twisting around, raising his submachine gun to end David's life, when a shot came from the west, the far west, and punched right into his head. The SMG flew from his hands. David snatched it out of the air, turned and unloaded into the three nearest Marauders, hosing them down with bullets and spraying their blood into the air.

"Get Cait out of here!" David screamed as he abandoned the now-depleted gun, sprinted over and scooped up a pistol that had been abandoned. He glanced back and saw that Lara was in the process of grabbing the knife the leader had dropped. She rushed over behind Cait and began cutting away at the ropes holding her.

"Fuck that! Get me a gun!" Cait yelled.

A lot of guns were opening fire now. From the west *and* the east, as well as to the south, where his people were.

Almost all of the guards that had been ringing the posts were now dead or dying. David shot one man in the head as he tried to draw a bead on them while simultaneously ducking the incoming fire, then yelled in surprised pain as a round punched him in the gut, his armor just barely standing up to it.

He twisted and fired four rounds into the last surviving nearby Marauder, shooting him three times in the chest armor, and then once in the neck. As he dropped his weapon and his hands began to go for his throat, a bullet suddenly exploded through the side of his skull and finished the job. David hurried forward and snatched up an assault rifle.

As he did, he saw Cait and Lara rushing over to join him.

"Babe, we *have* to get you out of here!" he yelled.

"Goddamnit, David! This is my home too and I'm fighting for it!" she screamed. "Now hand me that fucking rifle."

He looked at her for just a second, then issued a short, wild little laugh, then scooped up a rifle on the ground and handed it to her. "Goddamn I love you."

She grinned fiercely. "I love you too, dear. Now let's go finish this."

David looked out over the central settlement. It was chaos, but chaos in his favor. The Marauders, who had just thirty seconds ago held an overwhelming advantage, suddenly found themselves on a level playing field.

Hell, it was getting worse for them by the second. Ellie and Akila and the others had come through, he saw as he looked to the east and west. Two groups of people, all armed, were coming out of the woods and either hanging back and sharpshooting or rushing forward under the cover that the sharpshooters were providing.

The same thing was now happening to the south as the people from Haven attacked.

It felt very appropriate, given that the fuckers had done this exact same thing to them when they had first attacked.

David, Lara, and Cait set off, each holding a weapon with some ammo to spare that they had collected among the immediate dead. Most of the Marauders seemed to have fallen back towards the large mansion David had been intending to turn into their new headquarters. It made the most sense of anything, but he had no intention of letting them have it.

He saw his and Val's and Lori's people duking it out with some Marauders in the section of the settlement they had managed to set up during that week of work, with the Marauders clearly trying to fall back to the mansion, and his people having absolutely none of it.

David opened fire as he saw a group of Marauders making for the front gate. Cait and Lara immediately joined in and four of the Marauders wilted under a hail of gunfire. They were forced to fall back behind the nearest structure as several Marauders inside the mansion fired at them from out of second and third story windows.

"Fuck, I've been waiting to do this for days!" Lara roared as she reloaded.

"We have got *so* much catching up to do," Cait said as they hid behind a house, side by side.

"I know. God, it's been so fucking hard to be away from you," David replied. He grimaced as more pain assaulted his body. He wanted to give up, to just lay down and let the others take care of it, let them finish this. He was so tired, so hungry, so thirsty, in so much pain. He was absolutely exhausted at this point.

"Maybe you should be the one to get to safety," Cait said uncertainly, staring at him. "God, you look awful babe."

"I feel like shit," he muttered. "But I'm not done yet."

He took a moment to steady himself, then leaned carefully out from behind the house to get a view of the situation. The last of the Marauders had made it into the courtyard surrounding the mansion, the rest were dead or in the process of dying.

There couldn't be that many left. He saw several in the windows, most of which were now broken out, firing on the others. Cursing, he took aim with his rifle, held it steady, zeroing in on the face of a man who was trying to murder one of his friends, and squeezed the trigger the moment he had a shot.

Perfect headshot.

The man went down, half his head torn away by the bullet.

Immediately return fire stabbed out at him and he pulled back.

"Shit, we're going to need to get past that gate," he said.

"Get me a shotgun and I can get us past," Lara said. He wasn't sure he'd ever seen her so pissed before. Not that he blamed her.

"Almost certainly one among the more populated area," David replied. "We'll need to get there anyway, this place is too exposed."

"Let's move then," Cait said.

They headed along the back of the house, moving in the opposite direction, and started making their way towards the others. David was finding it increasingly difficult to keep focus. After all this time, all this effort, everything he had gone through, he was *finally* with Cait again. And there was no time for even a kiss or a hug. But they were close. They were so close. Just a few dozen more assholes to kill and they would be *done.*

As they slipped down another alley between a pair of houses, he began seeing others, some tending to wounded, some gathering weapons. A blue-furred figure skidded to a halt at the head of the alley, turned, and began to raise a weapon, then immediately relaxed.

"David! Cait! Lara!" Ellie cried, stepping into the alleyway. "Holy shit, you're okay!"

"Tell me that was you who shot Stern in the head," David replied.

"Yes, that was me," she replied.

"I always knew you'd be the one to kill that son of a bitch if anyone was gonna," Cait said. "Oh it's so good to see you, Ellie."

"I'm all for reunions but can we get a move on?" Lara asked.

"Yeah," Ellie said.

They hurried out of the alleyway and Lara looked around for a moment before finding a discarded shotgun, checking it out, and then beginning to march on the mansion. David and the others quickly followed in her wake. At this point, the others had it surrounded, and Ruby and no doubt a few others were keeping their distance, firing at any targets of opportunity they could find among the windows.

It wouldn't be long now.

By the time they got to the mansion, they didn't even have to make much of a dash across the open space, as the surviving Marauders had fallen back away from the windows.

"Make way," Lara growled as she stalked up with the shotgun.

The people around the gate made way and she blew the locking mechanism right out of the wood, then kicked in the two doors that made up the gate in the privacy fence surrounding the mansion. Immediately, they all flooded the courtyard. David led the charge with Lara and Ellie. As they hustled up the steps to the front door, a Marauder with a machine gun appeared, took aim, and promptly got his head blown off by Lara's shotgun.

After that, it was basically just a sweep and clear operation.

They flooded into the mansion, putting down Marauders wherever they found them. They stalked from room to room, down every corridor, checked every closet, every side room, and blew holes in the dark-armored bastards without hesitation. All in all, it took an hour to make sure that the mansion was clear. When the last room had been cleared, David found himself in a bedroom on the third story with Cait, Ellie, Akila, and Lara.

"That's it," Cait said, then groaned and sat down heavily on the bed. "Oh wow, I need a break. Shit, I'm not cut out for this anymore."

"We should clear the houses, all the buildings out there," Ellie said.

"Yes, it's going to take us weeks to clear the woods and make sure they're truly gone," Akila murmured.

"And almost certainly more of them will be coming," Lara said.

"I know," David said wearily, walking slowly over to a nearby floor-to-ceiling window that had somehow survived the whole ordeal. He looked out over the settlement, the fields and forests around it, the river, all the people out there. "We'll secure the region again, but for right now, we did it." He smiled tiredly and turned back to face them. "We did it."

EPILOGUE

David came awake, opening his eyes in darkness.

For a few terrifying moments, he had no idea where he was, or what he had been doing before going to sleep.

Someone was near him, against him, actually. Warm, soft.

He could hear soft respiration.

He blinked a few times, and finally it clicked home. Slowly, he relaxed. He *was* in a somewhat unfamiliar place, but that was fine. He was safe.

David was laying in his bed in the second story of the mansion in their new settlement. The place they had finally given a name.

Sanctuary.

He turned his head, saw Cait and Lara laying to one side. Beyond them, on another mattress pushed up in between the edge of their bed and the wall, Ellie and Ashley lay curled up together, sleeping peacefully. Turning to his other side, he saw Evie's bare back. He knew April was on her other side, hidden from view by Evie's large frame.

They were all sleeping, all safe, all here with him.

It had been three days since that final assault on Sanctuary.

They had been a long but mostly deeply satisfying three days.

They had spent the rest of that first day clearing the settlement, making sure there were no surviving Marauders hiding among the houses. They found two and shot them without hesitation. After everything that had happened, there wasn't room for mercy in them, not now. When Sanctuary was clear, David and Ellie took a detachment of people and went to make sure Haven was okay. The farmers and fishers, who had come through fully, had gone back to their own homes to make sure everything was still okay there.

Haven was safe, and the people were recovering, he had been happy to find.

That first night, he'd had sex six times, somehow. Mostly with Cait, but also with Lara and Jennifer, who had missed him terribly.

On the second day, they had decided it was safe enough to get people back, and he, Ellie, Akila, and Azure had gone to see Helen and begin the process of getting people back from the island. Part of him had been terrified that something had happened, but he'd sent a runner almost as soon as the battle was over to Helen to check on her and the people on the island, and the man had returned with good news: they were still safe.

While getting everyone back home and dealing with all the new corpses, they had taken the time to count their dead.

In the end, eight people had been killed in Val's group, and fifteen had died from Haven.

It was a monumental loss, given their population barely broke fifty before all this had happened. They spent all the rest of that second day gathering the dead.

At the beginning of the third day, they'd had a funeral, burying the dead in their now unfortunately largely expanded graveyard outside of Haven.

They tossed all the Marauders into a mass grave, burned their corpses, and then buried whatever was left.

Then they'd spent the rest of the third day just

helping people and making sure that everyone was getting to where they wanted to be, and were getting whatever supplies they needed. It would take time to get everything back on track, but they were already getting there.

When the sun had begun to go down, David had come to bed and passed out.

He'd been woken by Cait once, perhaps an hour, maybe two, after that, and they had made love. Although as horny as she was, she had been so exhausted that she had actually fallen asleep in the middle of the lovemaking session.

He'd finished shortly after and then passed out again beside her.

Now, David lay awake in the darkness. Sanctuary was quiet. He knew Val and Lori were in the room above him, sleeping soundly hopefully. Akila and Jennifer were somewhere here as well. Azure had gone home to report in to her people, but promised to return, to help them some more, as there was a lot of ground to cover and places to check and make sure surviving Marauders weren't gathering somewhere.

Although he had the idea that if there were survivors, and there probably were, they had long since run far, far away.

Things were changing now.

Thatch and his people had formally committed to a full-on alliance, promising to be more involved in the community at large, and to commit more resources and people to future assignments. And apologizing for hesitating so often.

Murray had, surprisingly, stepped down from his role as leader of the fishing village. David was convinced that Ruby would step up, but she declined. Against all odds, Cole took over the position. David was still trying to figure that one out, given the fisher's and Lima Company's poor relationship in the past, but Ellie said that Murray and Cole had a shared history. It wasn't that David thought the man incompetent, if anything he thought he'd make a great leader. And apparently the people of the village were okay with it.

Maybe they just wanted someone to step up and start doling out orders after everything that had gone down.

Cole was good enough at that, and so far, he seemed to be doing a decent job.

The doctors were split up among the settlements now, but they had finally agreed to move their headquarters to Sanctuary. Katya and Vanessa were okay. He'd been worried about Vanessa, as he had somehow managed to go the entire campaign without seeing her, but she'd arrived there at the end, large and in charge as ever.

Catalina, Match, Lina, and Tennyson had begun to feel a bit like outcasts, but David wasn't having any of that. After a brief conversation, they'd been welcome at Sanctuary, and all four had agreed to live and work with them.

David and what the ladies sometimes called his 'inner circle', Evie, April, Cait, Ellie, Lara, and Jennifer, had all moved to Sanctuary. They had agreed to leave Lindsay and Robert in charge of Haven, as the couple had proven themselves time and again as community leaders. They had graciously accepted and were now living in his and Evie's and Cait's old room after he and Evie had broken down their custom-made bed, moved it to Sanctuary, and remade it. That had been a nice little project that he had enjoyed immensely after all the awful shit that he'd had to subject himself to over the past week or so at this point.

Rolling over, David curled up against Cait and closed his eyes, starting to drift off again.

The threat of the Marauders was still out there, not to mention whatever other dangerous things they didn't even know about.

No doubt there was a lot of hard, dangerous work ahead of them.

But they were ready for it.

ABOUT ME

I am Misty Vixen (not my real name obviously), and I imagine that if you're reading this, you want to know a bit more about me.

In the beginning (late 2014), I was an erotica author. I wrote about sex, specifically about human men banging hot inhuman women. Monster girls, alien ladies, paranormal babes. It was a lot of fun, but as the years went on, I realized that I was actually striving to be a harem author. This didn't truly occur to me until late 2019-early 2020. Once the realization fully hit, I began doing research on what it meant to be a harem author. I'm kind of a slow learner, so it's taken me a bit to figure it all out.

That being said, I'm now a harem author!

Just about everything I write nowadays is harem fiction: one man in loving, romantic, highly sexual relationships with several women.

I'd say beyond writing harems, I tend to have themes that I always explore in my fiction, and they encompass things like trust, communication, respect, honesty, dealing with emotional problems in a mature way…basically I like writing about functional and healthy relationships. Not every relationship is perfect, but I don't really do drama unless the story actually calls for it. In total honesty, I hate drama. I hate people lying to each other and I hate needless rom-com bullshit plots that could have been solved by two characters have a goddamned two minute conversation.

Check out my website
www.mistyvixen.com

Here, you can find some free fiction, a monthly newsletter, alternate versions of my cover art where the ladies are naked, and more!

Check out my twitter
www.twitter.com/Misty_Vixen

I update fairly regularly and I respond to pretty much everyone, so feel free to say something!

Finally, if you want to talk to me directly, you can send me an e-mail at my address:
mistyvixen@outlook.com

Thank you for reading my work! I hope you enjoyed reading it as much as I enjoyed writing it!

-Misty

Made in the USA
Monee, IL
12 January 2024